→ GARDEN PRIMITIVES

stories)

GARDEN
PRIMITIVES

Danielle Sosin

COFFEE HOUSE PRESS

Coffee House Press is an independent nonprofit literary press supported in part by a grant provided by the Minnesota State Arts Board, through an appropriation by the Minnesota State Legislature, and in part by a grant from the National Endowment for the Arts. Significant support has also been provided by The McKnight Foundation; Lannan Foundation; Jerome Foundation; the Target Foundation; General Mills Foundation; St. Paul Companies; Butler Family Foundation; Honeywell Foundation; Star Tribune Foundation; James R. Thorpe Foundation; the Bush Foundation; The Lila Wallace-Readers Digest Fund; the law firm of Schwegman, Lundberg, Woessner & Kluth, P.A.; and many individual donors. To you and our many readers across the country, we send our thanks for your continuing support.

Coffee House Press books are available to the trade through our primary distributor, Consortium Book Sales & Distribution, 1045 Westgate Drive, Saint Paul, MN 55114. For personal orders, catalogs, or other information, write to: Coffee House Press, 27 North 4th Street, Ste 400, Minneapolis, MN 55401. coffeehousepress.org

"The Only Course" originally appeared in *Alaska Quarterly Review.*

COVER + BOOK DESIGN Kelly N. Kofron
COVER PHOTO © Earl Kendall / Kendall Photographs
AUTHOR PHOTOGRAPH Georgina Frankel

Library of Congress Catologing-in-Publication Data
Sosin, Danielle
    Garden primitives: stories/Danielle Sosin.
        p. cm
    ISBN 1-56689-100-0 (alk. paper)
        1. United States—Social life and customs—20th century—Fiction. I. Title.

PS3569.O714 G3 2000
813'.6—dc21
                                                                    99-086398

10 9 8 7 6 5 4 3 2 1
first printing / first edition
Printed in Canada

→ Contents

"Cézanne, for instance, starts to look at the cup before him with *both* eyes, opening one and then the other, and painting his doubts."

—David Hockney

→ *Ice Age*

"PERMANENT PLAGUE," Gil mutters, as he swings around the tractor and sets his disk in the sideviews. Worse than corn borers 'cause you can't use chemicals. Worse than drought 'cause hell's bet it'll rain someday. He shakes a cigarette loose from his pack and holds it in his teeth until the lighter clicks out. He never imagined it would go this far, them slapping up houses as fast as toolsheds, filling the whole southern half of his valley. City idiots. They brought the crime and the blacks down on themselves. What ever happened to reap what you sow? If he had his say he'd build the city sky-high, let them all live like chickens stacked in cages. Shit. Gil exhales a thick stream of smoke that mushrooms against the windshield of his cab, obliterating, if only for a moment, the sea of gray-roofed houses in front of him. There's a thought. Where's the old Enola Gay when you need her?

It's 7 A.M. and the traffic is up. Cherokees. Troopers. Ford Rangers. Waiting in line. Blinkers flicking. The sign above them at the stone wall entrance reads, "Fox Hollow Estates . . . The Best Of Both Worlds." If things were straight, Gil spits out the window, their cars would be axle-deep in Bill Jorgenson's field.

"You know how this back has been eating at me." Two seasons gone by, and Gil can still see the way Jorgenson looked. His face sagging as if he'd already lost some of what he'd been made of. And Jorgenson hadn't come around the car, but instead, kept six feet of steel between them. "Dana's pushing to move near the grandkids." Gil had stood silently nodding, popping the joint in finger after finger. No sense in saying anything, Jorgenson knew exactly how he felt. Knew him well enough to read his gestures. He didn't watch the green Chevy back down the drive, but went around the shed and fired up the chain saw. Jorgenson could read the sound of that too.

As Gil nears the south end of his field, he toys with the notion of not stopping. He could run her through the ditch, right on over County Road 18, punch his throttle to the floor, and land his tractor in someone's family room. The thought sets a chuckle gurgling in his throat.

He finishes out his row and turns back north, into the landscape he's known all his life—the pine windbreak off to the northwest, planted by his grandmother when they first got the deed, when the farm was only 160 acres and the "J" in Johnson was still pronounced as a "Y." Now, his stead runs a full 480. The clumped black dirt pocked with last season's cornstalks stretches ahead of him defining his weeks of work. Butting against his land, the Platt farm. Jerry Platt's gray clapboard house, hardly visible with the leaves coming in. Beyond the Platts', the tail end of Wilkens's place, its low spot where water stands in wet years, then the land rising up to meet the sky. There, the swaying line of his horizon that forms the shape of a hog's back, the same hog his father knew, the same, his grandfather.

First it was the rich folks buying up the river bluffs, then the small towns busting their seams, the developers scrambling to buy every scrap piece of land in the thirty miles between the river and the city. Used to be that land had a real value, based on what the soil could produce. But the figures on his land keep rising like floodwater, the taxes going up and up, and what's he supposed to do, squeeze twice the yield? Even so, he'd had a bellyful for any greedy bastard who'd agreed to sell. Rolls of bills where their balls should have been.

That was before his farm held the front line. Up close, he could see reasons more than money why a man might roll over. It was the air that was all wrong, packed full of things that didn't belong. The on-and-on racket of lawn mowers. The smell of a hundred barbecues.

Ice Age

Come night, their streetlights blocking out his sky. Not that it was going to make him roll. He'd be stiff as a plank when they got his land.

But now, on top of that whole stinking pile, he has got the fact of the other day to reckon with. He has got the fact of the dinosaurs. Gil sets to concentrating on the disk in his mirrors to keep the whole thing from unnerving him again.

It happened on Wednesday. A slow southerly wind. Gil was standing in his field, watching the sky like he'd done all his life, when he felt an emptiness blow through the valley. Felt it unbalance him like a whiskerless cat. Farming, he'd figured, was a private life. This, to him, was a point of pride. Thing was, through all those days of work, when he'd stop and scan the sky for weather, hoping for rain clouds or hoping against them, there had been part of himself that he'd never known, that relied on Jorgenson doing the same. The fact of rain, or the fact of blue sky, had connected every man in the valley, bound their fates, thicker than blood. It came to him quick as a razor cut. Extinction. Wiped out. Just like the dinosaurs. A slow south wind pushing gray clouds and he felt himself being pushed along with them, though there were his boots sunk in the dirt. He could hear his heart drumming hollow in his ears, feel his breath push against his spine. Ribs widening. Stretching long. His own bones, heaving into hard plates.

Gil tilts his head, stretches his neck until it releases with a pop. At least the dinosaurs never knew what hit them. He ends his pass and turns back south, trying to shake the whole thing off. But he sees it, sixty-five million years back, a meteor the size of his valley, slamming into some ocean, raising walls of water, volcanoes erupting all over the place. Then, the death blow, the dust and ash, blocking out every last piece of sunlight.

No, he doesn't blame the others like he used to, knowing now how it is to have them in his face, honking and waving at him out in the field as if he were some kind of novelty. The others must have felt it too.

Gil runs a hand over his stubbled head and tugs the bill of his cap back snug. The real son of a bitch is Heim. Just the sound of his name works on his last nerve. His selling was the strike of the match. The rest of them burned like a stand of dry pine. Rassmussens. Rudes. Hinkleys. Smithsons. If he could get his hands on Heim. Destroyed the past and the future all in one.

He can't let it get to him. He should set his thoughts on the work at hand, let his mind drop down into that slot that's like thinking, but not. More like cruise control. With spring so late, he'll be doing dog-time as it is. Being in the field is what he'd itched for. Days on end, the snow falling, while he watched Clint, or girly movies on cable, rereading back issues of *National Geographic*. Record-breaking accumulation. Couldn't see over the drifts from all the plowing he'd done. Even had to start piling it out back of the shed. Damn it if some isn't still there, a stubborn, dirty, icy mound, the kind that cuts your hands like saw teeth.

The houses loom larger as Gil nears, crazy-angled rooftops spilling down the valley. A jigsaw puzzle with every piece gray. In the road, a young girl racing on a bike. A lady lagging a distance back with another kid strapped in behind her seat. The girl flying smack down the center, weaving between the white lines, and the truck coming fast over the hill.

Gil's fist hits the horn. Sun flashing off spinning spokes. Purple bike. Pink shirt. The girl swerving to the side. The truck wrenching back on course. The girl falling silent as a downed bird.

"Holy fucking shit," Gil shouts over the blaring horn, his fist still slammed into it. The lady rushing up to the girl. The girl's leg bleeding all down her sock. With his heart pounding, he rounds out his turn. The lady, in his rearview, holds her hand up toward him, then lowers it to the base of her throat. "This isn't a playground," he yells over his engine, but the lady continues to wave at him.

Gil shuts down in the middle of the field and lays his head against the seat to give his heart time to slow. The sudden quiet hovers around him. Complete morons. Flaming idiots. He lights a cigarette and fills his lungs,

Garden Primitives

blows smoke at the roof of his cab. The sun barely to nine o'clock, and he's never seen the likes.

The light angles thick across the hog's back. A faint cloud of dirt hangs in the distance. Wilkens. Likely just going about his business. Relaxing. Having a hell of a morning. His mind getting to go wherever it wants. That's the way it used to be. Simple. Get up. Get yourself moving. No distractions. Just step up to the day. It's those kinds of things he'd taken for granted. Didn't know he had them till they were gone.

Christ. Those had been Aggie's words. Gil fires the engine and sets back to work. He hates to hear her voice in his head. He sees her, how she'd appeared in the doorway. He, smack in the middle of his bath. A suitcase in her hand, and Janey standing behind her. The hag. He'll never forgive her that exit, buck naked and to his waist in water. At least he'd had clothes on when Irene left. Both of them harping the same song. Lout. Stingy. And who knows what else. Finding his magazines ripped in half and thrown all over the front porch. All the trouble it took to replace them. And Aggie always bringing his age into things. What did she think, he could stop the seasons and wait for her to catch up to him?

Thank God he's over that hump, though sometimes he wonders what Janey'd be looking like. Hell, what was he supposed to do, show up in court and hang his business out in public? She'd be eighteen by now. Somewhere in Oklahoma, and who knows what kind of lies Aggie pushed on her. Hasn't heard boo in eight years. Eight years is long enough for anything to scar over.

Back then, too, it was the air that threw him. No taste of frying wafting out to the porch. No rose-smelling steam fogging the bathroom mirror. No sound of Jane practicing piano, or floorboards creaking over his head. Dead air. Emptiness. Things that were supposed to be floating around weren't. It was about subtraction then.

Gil flips on a call-in show. They're talking about building a dog track, yes or no? He works his row, turns up another, loses himself, finally hitting his rhythm. Calls from Lakeville. Winona. Star Prairie. Not that he leans either way. You won't find him out there wasting his money. No question, if they build it, it will be full-up. The same fools who go in for those lottery tickets. He sees 'em at the grocers, forking it over, picking their numbers from birthdays and whatnot, knowing all the while the odds are the same they'd be hit by lightning while tying their shoes.

The sun has reached near as high as it will, dropping thin-edged light all around. Gil notes the time and that the north sky has grayed. He watches an arrow of geese pass over, watches their dirt shadows trail across the field, then follows their direction back toward the house.

There's leftover roasted chicken and rice, and chocolate pudding that he'd made that morning. The whir of the microwave turns in his ears while he picks a fork from the can by the sink. He eats in the kitchen, heaping mouthfuls, while watching his show on the portable.

"Geology for eight hundred," the freckled lady says.

Gil sets the entire bowl of pudding in front of him and delicately skims ribbons of skin with a spoon.

"What is a kettle?" Gil says, before the contestants have hit their buttons.

"What is a kettle?" the freckled lady says.

"No, I'm sorry. That's incorrect. Doug? Jennifer? Time's running out. I'm sorry. The correct answer . . . What is a drumlin? 'Drumlin' is the term we're looking for."

"Bullshit," Gil says, and moves to the living room taking his bowl of pudding along. He punches up *Jeopardy* on the big screen and riffles through a pile of magazines. January's issue. "Glaciers on the Move." He runs his spoon down the columns of print until he finds the passage he's looking for. *The glacier left myriad lake basins behind . . . long sinuous ridges of stream-deposited gravel called "eskers"; ice-block potholes called "kettles"; and curious ice-molded hills called "drumlins."*

"Shit. Goddamn." Gil kicks the coffee table. He mutes the TV so he can reread. Most of the article he remembers, how it said that the ice age hadn't really left, that it keeps coming back, reasserting itself, and that people

Ice Age

today think this warmth is normal, when really, geologically, it'll last a short time.

He is reading about the properties of ice—that unlike almost every other substance, it is lighter as a solid than as a liquid, that it produces heat while freezing and absorbs it while melting—when he feels the air shift with another presence, and sees a lady through the oval front-door glass.

"Hi. Excuse me. I hope I'm not interrupting." She looks at the spoon in his hand. "I had to come over and thank you in person. My daughter. She's okay."

Gil sees tears in the lady's eyes and realizes she's the one on the bike. She stands half a head taller than he. A looker, with a long dark ponytail.

"She took off so fast, and I couldn't catch up to her. Her leg and her arm are scraped up pretty bad, I gave her some Tylenol and she slept a couple hours. I don't know how we can ever thank you enough, my God, that was so close, I keep seeing it in my head, if you hadn't been there . . ." She starts to cry.

"No bother," Gil says and starts to close the door.

"Wait, I'm sorry," she says, wiping her cheeks. "My husband is stopping for groceries on his way home from work. We really hope you'll come for dinner, he wants to thank you in person, he said, and here, Julie drew this for you. I hope six-thirty isn't too late, you'll come, won't you? If you hadn't been there, oh, God. I promise I'll have stopped crying by then."

Gil stares at the pink construction paper in his hand. He didn't even have time to get a word in, to say yes or no about supper before she ran off. It's a crayon picture of a man in overalls. Near him stands some sort of animal. A cow, Gil figures, too big for a dog. Around the man's head there's a yellow circle with lines reaching out like a sun. "Thanks for bloing your horn and saving me! Julie." On the back, in looping pen it says, Sue and Jeff Mackey. 6:30. 16459 Fox Den Lane. He drops it on the table and goes back to his reading.

Gil surveys the sky from his back stoop, then bends to double knot his bootlaces. He picks up his thermos, pats his pocket for smokes, and walks back into the field. A cool wind is blowing out of the north. He stops and turns his nose to it. No smell of rain. Good. His body feels old climbing up to the cab, and the door heavy, as he swings it shut. Better hit the coffee now if he's gonna make the afternoon. He pours from the thermos to the cup between his knees, lights a smoke, sets his disk, and starts back in. The entire sky has clouded over, blanketing the valley with a quiet weight. The woods on the bluff have a hunkered-down look, and the houses, too, the windows dark blanks, as if everyone over there were taking a nap. Of course, he's not going into one of them places. It would be like having tea with the Japs in '45. What's he supposed to do, just walk right over there? Gil throttles down and sweeps back north.

Ice Age

They've done nothing but run over everything he has known. Can't remember the last time he heard an eagle. And all those stores they brought along with them. The latest, shit, he could hardly stand his eyes. A store, had to be five acres, with nothing in it but garbage for house pets.

At least the developers had quit sniffing around. He rubs his cheek and chuckles, remembering the look on the last one's face.

"Please, Mr. Johnson, can't you give me five minutes?"

"Haven't got five to spare."

"They warned me you had your mind made up, but I said, 'You let me talk to him.' I'm sure an intelligent man like yourself never makes a move without weighing his options."

A new tactic, Gil thought, to send out a female. Not a bad shape to her at that. Creamy skin. Nice set of Dollies.

"Five minutes," he'd said, and let her in the front room. He watched her take stock of his surroundings, could almost hear the gears turn in her mind.

"I see you're quite a reader," she smiled, nodding toward his stacks of magazines. *"National Geographic* is one of my favorites."

Gil sat on the sofa with his arms crossed, smirking. She hadn't said a thing about the *Playboy*s.

"I'm not a man who likes being buttered, Miss. Four minutes."

She laughed nervously and shifted in the chair, galloping pink nails against the armrest. The nails reaching into a briefcase. Spreading papers on the coffee table between them. Gil spotted the open button on her blouse right away, and the low-cut, lacy, peach-colored bra that clasped at the base of a long cleavage line. She straightened and her blouse closed. Gil picked up the papers and held them at arm's length.

"I'm waiting on a new set of glasses. You'll have to help me out."

"Of course, Mr. Johnson. Can I call you Gilbert?"

"What's this?" he kept asking, so she had to lean over. He could tell she thought she was getting to him, by the way her voice started humming perky.

"You see what this could mean for your retirement goals, Gilbert?" she was saying when her eyes finally caught where he was staring. And how the red blotches rose up on her neck when she realized that he'd only been playing her.

A gust of wind shimmies his cab, joggling his brain back to what's in front of him. Dirt, rising off the old hog's back. It's not over. They'll send someone else. In time, they'll end up owning his land. Thing is he'll be dead so it won't be his worry.

Damn if he didn't forget his pills again. He can see the jumble of them on the counter where he left them. He rubs the vertical scar on his chest where they split

Ice Age

him open and rerouted everything. Ten years, he figures, he's got left on the place. And if luck keeps sleeping in his boots at night, the end, when it comes, will swoop clean like an owl. No way he's going to go out slow. Won't find him riding two wheels on the road like the rest of them down at the Walker Home. Could be the last thing he ever shoots is himself.

There's a tailwind now lifting dirt from his disk, sending it streaming along the ground out front. Gil sets the heat on low and watches a school bus out on 18. It turns in to the housing development, glowing yellow in the gray light, looking bright as a caterpillar. "Bloing your horn." What's that for spelling. He supposes he did save the girl's life. What were they thinking riding bikes out there. Someone ought to tell them what's what. They'll probably be taking nature hikes during hunting season, too. Sticking their hands down badger holes. Well, he can't be the one to take it on. They'll have to figure it out for themselves. Janey never did anything crazy like that. Broke an arm on the tire swing, but nothing stupid. It's the difference between being raised around a little common sense.

Gil watches a hawk circle, its stiff-winged body against the gray sky, banking, slowly climbing an updraft. Funny how little and white that cast was. And Janey planting herself on the sofa for days as if her leg were broken and not her arm. That little girl is sure to be laid up for a while. He pictures small legs tucked under an afghan, probably watching the afternoon programs, and drinking a bottle of 7UP. Likely they don't know enough to douse the cuts in iodine. Hell, it's hardly his problem to think about.

But the whole thing follows him up and down the field, all afternoon, breaking his rhythm, jumping up in his way like a yappy dog. What he needs is a hot bath and a whiskey.

Gil leaves his boots by the door, empties his thermos down the drain, and takes the whiskey bottle from the top of the fridge. Halfway up the stairs he sees the girl's drawing lying on the coffee table. "Ah, Christ," he says, trudging back down. The entire business just balled-up his day. He snaps up the picture, takes it into the kitchen, and drops it into the garbage can.

Clean trousers and a shirt and shave, he lights a cigarette and sits back with the remote. More sex scandals about the President. "Way to go," he says, toasting the screen with his lowball. It's the only thing he likes about the guy. Sure the economy's good, but none of that's thanks to him. It was the Republicans set it going straight.

In the kitchen, he flips on the other set and pulls a tray of pork chops from the freezer. He'll make boxed stuffing and canned baby peas. But instead of getting started on the fixing, Gil wanders back through the front room, opens the door, and steps onto the porch. He never uses his front porch anymore, though he used to appreciate sitting there at night, even after Aggie took Jane, and the porch swing just hung down empty. Now, of course, his view is spoiled. Somewhere over there they're expecting him to show. "To hell with it," he says, going back inside. He never agreed to anything.

The weatherman's talking about a cold snap, as if he can't feel it in the air. It's 6:22 by the mantel clock. He lights a cigarette and steps back outside, walks the porch slowly, testing boards for rot. A few of them are loose along their seams and spongy enough to give way to his nail clipper. Could be dangerous if anyone were racing around.

Gil transfers the pork chops to a plate and puts them in the microwave to thaw. When he goes to toss the blue styrofoam tray, the crayon farmer is looking right at him. A stain has soaked through around the cow from the greasy chicken bones underneath. He picks the drawing out of the trash and wipes it clean of coffee grounds.

The wind pushes against Gil's back, flapping his trouser legs as he walks down his drive. He fingers the bottle of iodine in his pocket. He'll hand it over and say good-night, tell them to stay off the road from now on.

County 18 is dotted with cars, most all of them turning in to the subdivision. Gil loiters by his mailbox and watches the road. No way he's crossing over if he recognizes anyone.

Once inside the Fox Hollow entrance, he checks the blurred pen of the Mackeys' address. There are roads branching off every which way like smooth-backed snakes on an even field of green. Robin Lane. Chickadee. Pheasant Drive. Oak Lane, with no oaks around. Nothing lying rusty. No dandelions.

Gil feels people eyeing him as he walks, but every time he turns to catch them, there's nothing there but milky drapes. The whole place makes his neck prickle up. It's the same damn sensation he gets at the doctor's when they make him sit waiting for an appointment. The way they plan out the carpets to match the chairs, everything done up to make you calm, when really it sets your bones grinding. 16459. What the hell kind of address is that anyway? Reads more like a phone number. He'd have driven if he knew it was going to be so far.

Fox Den Lane looks the same as the rest. The same big houses lining the road. The driveways leading up to double garages. How would a man tell the difference? Imagine, after a night of drinking, you could be halfway in bed with your neighbor's wife before you even realized where you were at. 16459. The house numbers climb at a slant by the door above a large pot of red and pink geraniums. Gil raises his fist to knock, but feels the legs of a wood tick crawling up his calf. He stoops to pull it out of his pant leg. Little fucker. He crushes it with his teeth and spits it into the flower pot.

"Mr. Johnson. I'm so glad you made it. I hope you weren't lost. I should have drawn you a map." The lady's hair is hanging loose, silky like those girls on the shampoo commercials.

"Come in. Please. I'm embarrassed to say that we started without you, but I guess we thought, well, that something had come up."

"I'm not planning to stay. I just brought by some iodine. You need to swab it on the girl's cuts. And stay off that road. It's not safe. And stay out of the woods come hunting season."

"Of course you're staying." The lady takes his arm and leads him into the entryway. "I made pasta and artichokes."

"Already eaten."

"Oh," she says, and then pauses. "Well please come sit with us. I made a strawberry tart especially in your honor."

Gil doesn't follow her. He stands on the rubber mat inside the door, looking at the ivory carpeting.

"My boots, ma'am. It'll look like shit on a snowfield if I cross over." The lady laughs a nervous little laugh.

"Sue, please. Can I call you Gilbert?"

"Name's Gil. How did you get it anyway?"

"What's that?"

Garden Primitives

"My name," he says. "How did you know my name?"

"Well, your mailbox," she says looking taken aback. "Wait, I'll get you a pair of Jeff's slippers."

Gil surveys the room while she's gone. There's a large chest like the one in his shed where he stores nails and bolts and such, but hers is sanded all smooth and stained. The furniture is beige and brown, everything looking like it has a place.

"Sorry about the mess," the lady says, nodding toward no mess that he can see.

Gil shuffles across the rug in the too-large slippers. How in the world did he get himself into this? He could really use a whiskey now.

"Julie, Gina, this is Mr. Johnson."

Two pairs of dark eyes look up at him.

"Hi, Mr. Farmer," the little one says.

"Hi. I mean thank you," the big one says shyly.

Gil eyes the gauze bandages on her arm.

"Please sit down." The lady motions to a chair.

He watches the kids pull leaves off of giant thistles. They dunk them in butter and pull them between their teeth. The door to the kitchen swings open and a man carrying a large platter walks in.

"Jeff, this is Gil Johnson."

Gil stands and shakes the man's hand, then sits back and slides his feet out of the slippers. It can't ever feel right wearing another man's shoes.

Ice Age

"I can't tell you how grateful we are," the man says. "I don't know what else to say but thanks. Can I get you a drink? Chardonnay? Merlot?"

"I could use a whiskey."

"Sorry. Beer?"

Gil looks across the table at the girl. He's a little surprised by her dark hair. He'd pictured her sandy-headed like his Jane.

"May I?" the man says reaching across the table.

Gil covers his plate with his hand. "No need. I've already eaten."

"Are you sure? Sue's famous for her marinara."

Gil watches him serve up plates of spaghetti with a thin red sauce, no meatballs or nothing.

"We just can't get over our luck," the woman says. "When I described to Jeff how it all happened, well it's so incredible, you being where you were. You were heaven-sent. A miracle. So now you have your own guardian angel, Julie. Not many people can say that."

Gil looks to the man to set her straight, but the man doesn't say anything. Of all the hogwash that people think. This kind of thing about does him in. Irene had a God way of seeing things too. Doesn't anyone read the papers? They just proved the Big Bang for crying out loud. What's the girl going to think, she's got some angel flying around that's going to stop her getting into trouble?

Gil takes a long swig of beer.

Garden Primitives

"I've never been a man for church. What you saw today's called plain coincidence, and I'm telling you that road's no place for horseplay, young miss." Gil feels the air go thick.

"How's your leg?" he asks the girl.

"It hurts," she says, "and now I can't be in my dance recital."

"Maybe if he's an angel he can get God to fix it so you can go anyway," the little one says.

"Missing a dance should teach you a lesson. I'd of tanned my girl's hide if she'd done what you did."

"What's tanning hide?" the little one asks.

"It means . . . ," the lady pauses, "It means punish, honey."

"Like a time out?"

"I brought this for your cuts," Gil says, placing the small brown bottle on the table. "After supper you'd better have your mother apply it. I'm not saying it won't hurt 'cause it will. It'll feel like you hit a hornet's nest, but it's the best thing against infection."

The girl's eyes grow wide as she stares at the bottle.

"I'll take another beer," Gil says.

The lady rises from the table, exchanging a curious look with her husband.

"So, Mr. Johnson. Have you lived around here long?"

"Me. My father. My father's father."

"That's fantastic," the man nods.

Christ. Gil turns his attention to the girl. "What grade are you up to in school?"

"I'll be going into fourth next year," she near whispers.

"Fourth, huh. Got a favorite subject?"

"I like adding," she says, twirling spaghetti onto her fork.

"Math? Well that's a solid subject. Maybe you can prove out the chaos theory one day. You know I used to have a little girl about your age, not much of one for math, but she could play the piano real pretty."

The girl raises her eyebrows and shrugs.

"Where is your daughter now?" the lady asks.

"Oklahoma's my guess, but hell if I know. I haven't seen her since my ex took off."

"He swore," the little one covers her mouth.

"So Gil, how are your crops doing?" the man asks.

"Ain't got no crops yet." Jeez, the guy must be an idiot. Doesn't he drive past the field twice a day? Gil takes out his pack of cigarettes.

"I'm sorry," the man says, as Gil shakes one free. "We don't allow smoking in the house. You're welcome to step out on the balcony."

Gil stands in the dusk in his stocking feet and shields his lighter from the wind. The sky has cleared and the air's cold. A shaft of dining room light falls across the wooden deck. Gil moves into the shadow. He can see into the neighbor's kitchen. It's got white wallpaper with specks of blue and a strip of yellow chickens going all around the top. He pulls on his smoke and shakes his head. He can't believe that sullen little girl is the same one who drew him the picture. He gauges the distance back home. From the lay of 18, and what he can glimpse of his field, he figures he's standing about at Jorgenson's barn. Raised voices come through the glass door. Gil flicks his butt over the rail.

"That may be true, but I expect you to behave," the man is saying as Gil slides the door open.

He takes his seat across from the girl, but she's keeping her eyes away from him.

"I gathered from the lay of things out there that your house is sitting where Jorgenson's barn was."

The girl stares at her plate, and no one says anything.

"I'll just finish this and be on my way," Gil says, giving a small salute with his beer.

"You mean cows, and pigs, and chickens lived here?" The little one fidgets in her chair.

"No. I didn't say that." Gil notes the disappointment cross her face. "I suppose you could count the deer," he says.

"Deer. They're my most favorite."

"Well, Bill ran a deer processing business in the fall. Used to dress them out right here."

"Deers don't wear clothes, silly."

Ice Age

"I'm not talking about clothes, I'm talking about dressing. He'd gut 'em, clean 'em, cut 'em into steaks."

The little girl's lip begins to wobble.

"You're lying," she cries, and runs from the table. The other girl pierces him with a hateful stare, pushes from the table, and goes after her sister.

Gil looks from the man to the lady, but neither offers any explanation. They just sit there all pale and quiet.

"Don't you teach your kids nothing? Shit." Gil slaps the table and stands.

"They're pretty young for that kind of talk," the man says.

"Talk?" Gil repeats, heading for his boots. "Hell. It's just a fact of life."

"I'm going to check on the girls," the lady says.

"Maybe it's just another way of looking at things," the man says, as Gil shoves his feet into his boots.

"Yeah, sure. Whatever you say."

"Look, we're thankful for what you did today."

"Thanks nothing," he says, opening the door. "It was reflex. I woulda done the same for a cat."

The wind gusts stiff and cold from the north, and the last light glows over the western bluff. The windows of the houses are all lit up. It's quiet. No one on the street but Gil. What the hell was he thinking to come here? Absolute morons, just like he'd always known. He can't seem to walk fast enough. House after house looks the same and he starts to feel like he's not really moving, but stuck in some revolving door. If he had his gun he'd shoot up the place, every streetlight and window; shit, he'd shoot up the grass.

Finally, he sees the stone wall entrance and the darkness beyond that is his field. Almost out. Almost free, he tells himself. But he doesn't feel free when he passes through. And he doesn't slow down when he reaches his drive; he's not sure he could if he wanted to; it's like the whole damn mess has settled in his boots, propelling his feet and who knows when they'll stop. He slams through his front door, grabs the whiskey from the table, and keeps on going, right out the back.

His boots sink into the newly turned soil and slow him to a labored trudge. Maybe he ought to just sell the damn place. Take the money and move far away. Florida, where it's warm all the time and there's no corn growing, no seasons at all. Maybe find himself some widow who likes to cook and who knows to keep her opinions to herself. He opens the bottle and tilts it to his lips, feels its heat wrap around his stomach. Why not? Some little place on the ocean. Take up fishing, lie around, watch movies all day.

A car door slams up at Platt's place. Gil stops to take another drink. Let Platt deal with it. After him, it'll be Wilkens. What does he care.

The whiskey's warming him now, doing its magic. A bat swoops near his head. Gil stops walking and looks at the sky. A half moon is climbing in the east. To the northwest is the city's orange glow. And there, the Big Dipper, riding the hog's back. He stands a long time watching the hog and smoking, then turns around and heads toward his house.

He's not selling. He'll never sell. He wouldn't exist anywhere else, not in any form he'd recognize. At least he's smart enough to see it. Jorgenson will die before his time, not even knowing what got under his skin. "Sons of bitches," Gil hollers. He points his bottle at the sea of houses, leans his head back, and opens his throat.

The moon is throwing light on the roofs of his outbuildings and bouncing off the line of ice along the shed. Gil unzips his trousers and pees on the ice, carving out a steaming hole. A line of ice in June. Ain't that crazy.

A smile pricks the corners of his mouth, and he's zipping his pants walking back in the field. Glaciers. The smile inches across his face. It hasn't really left. A relatively short time. There, all the lit houses spread down the valley. Yes. He laughs and spins to the north, feeling the cold blow against his face, seeing the giant wall of ice bulldoze its way clear down the valley. And when it recedes it will all be new again. Yes. Goddamn it. Gil toasts the north wind. Fucking hell, bring on the ice age.

→ *Internal Medicine*

I SIT ON THE EXAMINATION TABLE, wearing a gown, fiddling with the blood pressure wall mount. Seriously, I'm not in the mood. There's a knock on the door and Dr. Hardy walks in, four students trailing behind in lab coats that look like they just came out of the packaging. This is all I need. Dr. Hardy. Or Hardly Dr. as most of us call him. He reminds me of a Santa gone bad, bushy white eyebrows, a bulgy red face. You wouldn't let your kid near his lap.

"Well, well," he says, patting my knee. "I haven't seen you in a long time."

I'd requested not to work with him.

"This is Laurel, your teaching model for today."

I wait for the next line.

"And I'm Dr. Hardy." He grins and runs his tie through his fingers. "Get it?"

The students don't get it. It wasn't in their lecture notes. They stand bunched in the farthest corner like a patch of newly sprung mushrooms. They clear their throats and look at the floor, nervous to the point of pale.

Being first-year med students, their only patient contact has been probing scopes in each other's ears and noses. Starting them off in women's health is, in my opinion, some idiotic form of hazing.

I don't know why I do it. It's different with nurses and nurse practitioners. Nurse midwives are gravy of the earthy brown variety. I guess I teach them out of charity, if you can call it that at $100 an hour. The problem is, I'm not feeling philanthropic. Not after last night.

"Did you have a good time?" I asked my seven-year-old, Shawn, who had come home from spending the weekend with his father. He informed me that they'd gone to the zoo, accompanied by a woman named Dee Dee who could growl exactly like a Bengal tiger. She'd cooked my son chocolate chip whipped cream pancakes.

"For dinner?" I asked.

"Jeez, Mom, breakfast."

"Go brush your teeth," I said.

Dr. Hardy is explaining the clinic's format. With Hardy I have to take control right away. First, by establishing eye contact with the students. I usually have to stare them down before they'll look directly at me.

As Dr. Hardy bumbles on, I interject clarifying comments. It's when I begin to finish his incomplete sentences that the students know who to pay attention to.

Garden Primitives

"So you'll each do a speculum and bimanual exam. You're lucky to have Laurel. She's an old pro."

The man needs to retire.

"Who's going first?" Hardy claps his hands as if someone had set a big steak in front of him. "Which one of you has the best GPA?"

There he goes, confusing them again.

"I will," says a young man shakily raising his hand. His plastic name tag reads *Brent*. He's got the look of breeding and young entitlement that makes me cringe. But he's so nervous that beads of sweat are already forming at his temples. It's a good sign. The few that aren't scared are the ones to worry about. The ones who should go into surgery, since they've already got the cocksure attitude.

I lie back, put my feet in the stirrups, and scoot my rear to the end of the table. Then I adjust the drape over my knees so I can see the young man's face. Someone has masking-taped a picture to the ceiling, presumably to help the patients relax. It's a silhouetted couple on a sunset beach, obviously torn from a travel calendar.

"You okay, Brent?" I ask. He nods mutely from his stool between my legs. "Don't worry," I say, lifting my foot from the stirrup. "One false move and I'll kick you in the head." I've shocked him, but finally got the others to laugh, except the big redhead, Matt, who is staring with seeming fascination at his shoe.

Internal Medicine

"Now where's the labia majora?" Hardy asks. The young man touches me with his gloved finger. "Good. And the labia minora? What about the mons pubis, the mound of Venus?" This one usually stumps them, but Brent must have studied. "And the clitoris?" Brent's probing around, but he's not even close. I'm astounded whenever this happens. You can bet the women always know where it is.

"What is this, Ralph? Chocolate chip pancakes?" I was in the car, heading to the clinic, using the cell phone I keep for emergencies. "You've got some stranger in the kitchen with my son, spooning whipped cream down his throat first thing in the morning."

"She isn't a stranger."

"What's that supposed to mean? No. Don't tell me. God, Ralph. Dee Dee? Sounds like one of those green birds that talk."

"Look. I'm human. I have needs."

"Your son's teeth have needs."

I can see his face going solid in anger.

"Breakfast is oatmeal," I hollered into the phone. "It's cornflakes." But Ralph had already hung up.

The students all have speculums in their hands. They open and close them, fiddle with the screw locks. The room is clacking, overrun by a litter of silver platypuses. Brent wipes his brow on his sleeve.

"Okay now, I'm just going to touch you," he says

and starts to inch his hand down my thigh.

"Stop," I say, and he rears back, eyes wide. "Two things. First, there is the temperature of the speculum. You need to check it either on your wrist or else against the woman's thigh."

"Oh yeah, sorry," he says. "I suppose you wouldn't want it too cold."

"Too cold is startling. It's too hot that's problematic."

"Oh, I hadn't thought of that," he says. "It's great that you're doing this. Are you in medicine?"

"No. I'm in debt."

My therapist says that for the past couple years I've been masking my anger and pain with product. Now, instead of running up my credit card, I stop at garage sales to buy twenty-cent plates. I have stacks of them in my furnace room where I send them smashing beautifully against the cement wall.

Brent starts with his hand again.

"That's the other thing. Look, you guys. I know they teach you that it's respectful to touch the woman's thigh before her genitalia, but really a simple touch will do. The itsy-bitsy spider routine is a little bit overboard, don't you think?"

Their heads swivel toward Dr. Hardy who digs his hands in his pockets and shrugs.

"I can assure you," their heads swivel back, "that Dr. Hardy has never been in this position."

Internal Medicine

I can feel the speculum blades open inside me.

"I think I've got it," Brent announces, meaning a view of my cervix.

"You'd better consult your colleagues," says Hardy, using his deep official voice.

There are four heads between my thighs, looking, nodding, maneuvering the light.

"All right, if you all agree," he continues. "Now's when you'd take your cultures, etcetera. This is one tool we use for the pap smear. You put it in and get your sample, rub it against a slide, and spray it with fixative."

All four heads nod.

"It's a little more complicated," I say. Do you all know where the os is? I'm not talking Emerald City. It's that small opening at the end of the cervix. The protuberance on the end of the paddle is inserted into the os, then turned in a circle to get a scraping of cells. You should also take a scraping from the outer area."

"Well, yes," Hardy stammers. "That's the procedure. We won't actually do it on Laurel."

"We certainly will not," I say flatly.

"Your next job, young man, is to remove the speculum."

Brent's eyes start to bulge. They're always afraid it'll clamp down on the cervix.

"Just do the reverse of . . . what you just did," Hardy says before turning away.

Brent looks directly at me.

"Unscrew the lock all the way," I say calmly. "Okay, now it's your thumb on the lever that's in control of the blade position. Ease off on the thumb, and as you pull the speculum back you'll be able to take a look at the vaginal walls. Take your thumb off, the blades will close on their own. Good." At this point he'd give me his firstborn.

I wouldn't trust myself with another child, not after the mess we've made of Shawn's life. I thought we'd given an assuring presentation the night we told him that Mommy and Daddy were going to live in separate houses. He crumpled to the floor as if his bones had broken all at once.

Now I have a seven-year-old with a pocket calendar. He's at my house, then Ralph's, in two-week shifts. The weekend between week one and week two, he goes back to whichever of us doesn't have him. He has two rooms, two beds, and two parents who barely speak to each other.

I notice a sudden silence in the room. Brent's face is screwed into confusion. When Hardy explains the bimanual, he turns his back to the students and puts his fist on the wall—his fist is supposed to be a uterus—then goes about demonstrating finger placement. All the students can see is the back of his head. Usually, I imitate Hardy's hand movements like a signer for the hearing impaired, but I missed my cue. I should have called in sick. Brent sits stiffly, his gloved hand in mid-air, two fingers smeared with gel.

"You do a bimanual standing up," I say. "Think of my body as a uterus." I bend my arms up to the sides like an infant's. "My arms are fallopian tubes. My fists, ovaries. Put two fingers in my vagina and slide them back until you feel my cervix. You feel it?"

"I'm not sure," Brent says apologetically.

"You can't miss it. It's the only thing in there. It'll feel cartilaginous, like the end of a nose."

The other students touch their noses.

"I got it," he says. "Awesome."

"Try to stabilize it with your fingers to either side. Now put your other hand on my abdomen. You want to get the uterus between your two hands to check for size and tenderness." He's able to do this relatively quickly.

"Wow, when I push down, I can feel it bump against my fingers."

"Yep," I say, "they're connected."

It's not like I want Ralph back. God, no. Not after what we went through. Ten years, and the last two felt like thirty. But then there was Shawn, our home, our history. I won't marry again. Not a chance. What sane person would consent to become a Siamese twin? Sure, sew us together at the torso. Anesthesia? We anticipate no pain. We'll stay close, we'll share the same heart.

How convenient, our privates are always within reach. We'll walk three-legged through the world with the sturdiness of a milking stool. So how to dismantle such a creature? I'll tell you, it's a dull saw in Solomon's hand. You're left with half a heart in the end, and the problem of figuring out whose leg was whose.

"Now what?" Brent asks, his fingers still in me.

Dr. Hardy isn't paying attention. He's telling his gynecological war stories. The twenty-nine–pound ovarian cyst. The obese woman who at seven months had no idea that she was pregnant.

"Put your fingers together like this," I tell Brent, holding my hand in the Brownie salute. Move them till they're to one side of my cervix. You're going to sweep down with your external hand toward where you're holding your fingers inside." I do the infant arm again and with my other hand sweep through the air, catching my fist on the way, pulling it down to where it bounces off my hip. "The trick is to catch the ovary as you go. The feeling can be as subtle as a flick against your fingers."

"Like this?" he says.

"Right, but you've got to press harder. There's fat, muscle. They're down there protected. Think of it like you're dragging a lake." Brent attempts a few more times. "Try the left one," I say, but he still isn't getting it. I can tell that he wants to keep trying, but I'm not running a ring toss here. He takes off his gloves and washes his hands. He looks happy and relieved, but like he could sleep for a week.

Dee Dee . . . Dee Dee. So Ralph's got a pet bird. Does he have to drag my son into it? It's bound to get him all confused. And what if Shawn gets attached to her and it doesn't work out? I worry about the examples we're setting, and how they might affect him later. Ralph's got two whole weeks to do whatever he pleases, or whoever he pleases I guess I should say. He can bring a different one home every night. A warbler. A screech owl. He can write his own scratch-and-sniff field guide.

"Who's next?" Dr. Hardy asks. "What about one of you gals?"

Michelle, blonde-banged, looks like she could still be in high school. She stands near my knee as she gloves up. "Hold on," I say. She looks at me quizzically. "Your nails." She fans her hand and looks with admiration. "You can't do a pelvic with nails like that." I watch the information sink in. In all the sacrifices she's undoubtedly prepared herself for, the debt, the long hours of residency, it had obviously not occurred to her that she'd have to give up her manicured nails. "Sorry," I say. "There's always psychiatry." She retreats to the corner and then leaves the room.

Dr. Hardy has stepped out to answer his pager. I can't help but feel for the babies he delivers. Straight from the womb to his long red fingers.

Vathima has seated herself on the stool. She has sleek black hair held up in a clip.

"Can we start without him?" Her accent is thick. "Not that he seems to be so much helping."

Her nervousness shows in her thin, trembling hands.

"Majora. Minora." She goes through the routine. "Mound of penis," she says earnestly. I cover my mouth and cough to keep from laughing.

"And what is it you're looking for?" I ask.

"Well, to make sure that everything has its place."

"Yes, but there are other things, too. Warts, lesions, signs of STDs."

So what. Ralph is over us just like that? I don't care, really, I don't. Dee Dee. I picture a giant parakeet sunning on his deck, pecking at a plate of seeds, with one of Ralph's "you should read" books lying open. I can see Dee Dee fluttering around his kitchen, brandishing a spatula as big as a plate. Chocolate chips. Whipped cream. Maraschino cherries.

"I can't see it," Vathima says, maneuvering the speculum.

"You don't have the blades open wide enough." I feel the pressure as she follows my instructions.

"My goodness, yes. It is just like the textbook."

There's a knock on the door, and Michelle comes back in, Dr. Hardy following behind. "Excuse me. That was my wife on the phone. She calls me from the middle of a paint store. Blue or beige for the bedroom walls? I tell her what's the difference? We're not awake."

Ralph is the only person I ever met whose eyes don't shut all the way when he's sleeping. I remember how unnerving it was in the beginning. His head on the pillow next to mine, just a slit of white and iris showing. You come to love the strangest things in a person. He used to sleep with his hand buried in my hair.

Vathima is ready to do her first bimanual.

"Are you okay?" I ask.

She nods and, wide-eyed, eases her small fingers into me.

I hear a tight ticking noise from the adjoining bathroom. Looking over my shoulder, I can see Michelle seated on the closed toilet seat. Her blonde bangs fall over a determined face as she clips her nails into the trash can. It's stunning really. I'm proud of her. It's like watching a novitiate shave off her hair in preparation for a life of celibacy.

Vathima can't feel my ovaries either. Dr. Hardy puts a hand over hers and presses down hard enough to cause internal damage. I rise up on my elbows and stab him with my eyes.

"Oops," he says.

Vathima is mortified.

I can't comprehend how Ralph can be dating. After ten years of marriage, just like that. After living through our train-wreck divorce: slabs of metal and flying glass, everything twisted beyond recognition. In my own slogging attempts at salvage, libido has not even made the list. Dee Dee . . . Dee . . . Dee. Unbelievable.

Matt is a big redhead with a homegrown look.

"Okay, okay," he says, sitting on the stool as if talking himself into jumping out of a plane. He touches his hand against my thigh. "Warts, right? FTDs?"

"Not unless you're planning on sending flowers."

"Please," he says, looking me steady in the eye. "I need your help."

You can tell right away when they've got the touch. It's deliberate and gentle, like their fingers care. I stare up at the couple on the sunset beach, their arms locked easily around each other's waists. I remember our trip to the Virgin Islands. I close my eyes against Matt's slow probing. Hot sand and the saltiness of beach skin. The light behind my lids blooms orange.

"My hands are too big."

"You're doing fine," I say quietly.

I see Ralph in bed, a sleepy smile on his face, green feathers stuck in his hair.

"I don't want to hurt you," Matt says. The back of my eyes are warm and buzzing. He spreads me open, his fingers exploring as if each one contained a small oval eye. "I was so nervous last night, I hardly slept," he says.

Internal Medicine

I see Ralph's arm reach across the sheets. His hand lands not on a bird, but on the flesh of a woman's waist. It slides to her hip. It slides down her thigh.

"This will all get easier though, won't it?" Matt asks.

I don't love him anymore. I don't care.

"Of all the exams, this is the one."

Shawn is my concern. What if he'd walked in on them?

"I mean the whole thing is so intimate."

I see Matt standing between my thighs, the speculum poised and ready in his hand. "Are you okay?" he whispers. "I'm so nervous."

"I'm fine," I say forcefully, rising up on my elbows. "Get ahold of yourself. This is not about sex."

❧ *What Mark Couldn't See*

CLOUDS GATHERED OVER THE CITY, snow-laden, dark, and dropping. They deepened the blue cast of dusk that glowed between tree limbs, lay over the snow, and filled the bowl of air held between the riverbanks. A dog loped on the frozen ice. It stopped, nipped at its hind leg. Knobby vertebrae showed through its thin, blowing fur. The clouds descended over the highway and over rectangular tracts of housing. City streetlights flickered on as did the yellow lights of dining rooms where children set out napkins for dinner. The clouds lay thick over the Lamberts' roof where the dining room globe light hung over the table, where a bowl of carrots was passed around, and where nobody mentioned Tammy.

Mark wanted to bring her up, to say, "Hey, it's Tammy's birthday today," as if he had just remembered it. On her last birthday she'd turned thirteen and was finally allowed to pierce her ears. They'd looked all sore and red, he remembered, though all through dinner she kept smiling, her fingers twisting the small gold balls. Everything was different now. Silverware poked mutely into soft piles of food. Mark chewed his pork chop slowly and avoided looking at Tammy's spot at the table, the dark stained wood, not even a place mat. In the yard, the blues of winter had vanished.

"No, we are not getting a guinea pig," Mark's father said to Cindy, who had been asking all week.

"Why not?" Cindy folded her arms. Mark stopped chewing and shot Cindy a look. Silence. A load of wash in the basement hit the spin cycle. "They're free, and Laurie has four babies," Cindy pressed on. Mark's father leaned over the table, his thin upper lip drawing tight across his teeth.

"I don't care if she has a hundred."

"For God's sake, Earl," Mark's mother intervened.

"Dad," Mark swallowed his half-chewed meat, "Who do you think is better, Worsley or Maniago?" But Cindy was crying; his mother fussed over her and glared at his dad across the table. Mark's father's face was hard; the globe light glinted off his glasses. He dropped his crumpled napkin on his plate and pushed his chair away from the table.

"Jesus Christ," Mark's father muttered, kicking aside scattered boots in the hall. The backyard cold wrapped around him. He gathered a load of firewood, the bark pinching into his forearm. Snow, he thought, looking at the sky. He wanted to flee, to jump in his car and drive for two days to the mountains. He wanted to carve sharp lines with his skis, feel speed on his cheeks, speed blurring the pines. Mostly he wanted silence, to hear only the hollow sound of wind in his ears.

"Just eat a couple," Mark's mother prodded, stabbing a carrot with her fork, holding it halfheartedly to Cindy's closed mouth.

Mark heard the den door bang shut. "Can I please be excused?" he asked.

"Your father didn't mean to snap."

Mark turned toward the window but all he could see was the room reflected back at him, Cindy, and his mom, with Tammy's place next to hers. Why can't they leave Dad alone, he thought.

"Mom, I'm done," he tried again.

"Fine, but clear the table first, will you honey?" Mark took his plate and then his father's. He balanced the salad bowl on top. Clearing had been one of Tammy's jobs. Mark couldn't see why she'd made such a stink about it. All you had to do was carry plates to the kitchen, which was better than taking out the garbage.

"She has always been difficult," his parents had told him, after they'd agreed to let Tammy live in a foster home. "We just can't control her; it's the best thing for everyone." And the house had settled down without her. There were no more truancy calls from her school, no more bouts of her running away or picking fights with his dad, who'd explode, and then everything would get crazy. Mark set the plates on the counter and went back to the dining room for more. Cindy was gone. He picked up her plate, still full of the mealy orange disks.

"Can I go skating?" Mark asked, knowing well enough that it was a school night, knowing too that in the past few months rules had seemed to fade from his parents' minds.

Mark's mother didn't answer, she was staring at the weave of her place mat. She was trying to conjure an image of Tammy sitting at someone else's table. I hope they have a birthday cake, she thought. She pictured Tammy's cheeks full of breath, and wondered what her daughter would wish for. Despite Earl's wishes, she had sent her earrings and a card that she'd signed with all of their names. Earl would be furious if he knew. She had wanted the family to take Tammy to dinner. "Damn it, Marilyn," Earl had said. "Stop catering to her. If she doesn't want to be part of our family, then fine."

"Mom, can I go skating?"

Boots. Scarf. Hat. Gloves. Mark hung his skates over his shoulder, put a puck in his pocket, and grabbed his stick. He closed the door on the thick smell of pork chops, stepping into the sudden cold where the snow lay knee-deep across the backyard. The quiet lace of winter surrounded him.

Garden Primitives

Mark's breath puffed out. He could see Mrs. Schuster washing dishes in her kitchen. High on a pole, the alley light buzzed; it lit the dirt-marbled snow that crunched under his boots. The McDooleys' house looked like a jack-o-lantern, he thought, with all the windows glowing orange. He considered stopping to see if Brian could play but then remembered that it was a school night. The Mersers' dog, Pepper, started barking, running crazy along the fence like she always did. Mark rapped his hockey stick over the wood boards. Whap, whap. Pepper worked herself into a frenzy, jumping up on her short legs, sticking her nose between the slats, growling like she was some kind of tough dog.

The playground behind the school was empty, trampled with boot prints that went every which way. The school looked creepy at night, Mark thought. All was quiet except for the crunch of his footsteps and the rope that clanged against the flagpole. He imagined the school's deserted hallways, every locker closed, classroom doors shut. He could picture the gym, the thick climbing ropes motionless, no squeak of tennis shoes against the polished floor. Crunch, crunch. The hollow clang.

Mark's sixth-grade classroom was on the second floor. Inside were all their papier-mâché masks that Mrs. Larson had hung above the blackboards. He knew they were up there in the dark, staring over the rows of empty desks, all the chairs turned upside down.

What Mark Couldn't See

Mark hated that Mrs. Larson knew about Tammy. One day at recess she'd held him back while everyone else filed outside. "I hear you're having some problems at home . . . How are you doing?" I'd be doing better outside, he'd thought, but told her it was for the best and that he was fine, thank you. Still, Mrs. Larson wouldn't let it drop, pinning him with knowing sad looks just about every day. Mind your own dumb business, Mark thought, and swung his stick toward the dark windows, an imaginary puck flying toward the glass.

The street between the school and the park was busy. Mark stood waiting on the curb. Small icy snowflakes were falling; he could see them in the headlights of the oncoming cars. He knew he should go to the corner to cross, but instead dashed out through a pause in the traffic, his skates flopping against his body as he ran. Brakes squealed. A man glowered through his windshield and shook a scolding finger at him.

The lights inside the warming house were bright. Mark took in its familiar smell, a mix of floor cleaner, rubber, and cola syrup. He found a spot on a bench with an empty boot-cubby. There were three teenage girls across from him, popping gum while they laced their skates, the white kind, with pom-poms and bells. One thing about Tammy, he thought, at least she wore hockey skates. Of course, there had been a huge fight in the store, his father wanting Tammy to get the white ones, his mother waffling, then taking her side. Mark remembered the fat woman at the register, staring at them like they were a freak show. He'd crossed the aisle and gone to the tennis section pretending to be interested in rackets.

"Ets-lay o-gay," the tallest girl said, looking straight at Mark who hadn't realized he was staring. He ducked his head and pulled at his laces. The girls shoved their skate guards under the bench and passed around lip gloss. As if he couldn't understand them, Mark thought. As if he even cared what they said.

"Et-gay ost-lay," Mark mumbled at the blast of cold air and the metal door catching shut.

Mark balanced on his skates down the plywood stairs, each scored with blade cuts. He pushed onto the rink with a confident glide, felt the icy air rush over his face. The snow had stopped though the sky looked thick, hanging close above the floodlights. There weren't many people out except the Richfield High School team practicing in the hockey rink. Mark skated along the boards, pushing his puck out in front with his stick. The players swirled around each other. He listened to their skates scrape and scratch the ice. Mark could see their eager blades. Backward. Cross-step. They called to each other. Quick-stop. Whomp. The puck cracked against the boards, and the players knotted in the corner.

Mark started on his laps, skating hard while handling the puck. He skirted the hockey rink, left it behind, heading for the far end of the ice that he and Brian called The Mine Field because the ice was bumpy and dimly lit. He maneuvered through the rough ice, curved back along the tennis court side where Jane McDonald had got her tongue stuck, frozen to the chain-link fence. Back to the warming house, home base. Up along the hockey rink again, to the no-man's land of The Mine Field. Around and around he lapped, imagining that the hockey coach noticed him, noticed how well he handled the puck, his concentration, determination. He imagined the man nodding to himself in approval.

Mark coasted to center rink. Warm and breathing hard, he unzipped his jacket. He picked up the puck and dropped it to the ice. Face-off. Mark wrestled the puck from his opponent, juked around him, and headed for The Mine Field. *He dodges players left and right. It's Lambert with the puck. He fades right, over the blue line. He cuts, reverse, down in the corner, crossing out in front of the net. He shoots. He scores!!* Mark lifted his stick over his head, saluting the crowd which was on its feet cheering.

"I'm going now," Mark's mother said, standing in the doorway to the den. Mark's father looked up from the television. She had fixed her hair and changed blouses. He could smell her good perfume. He turned his wrist, looked at his watch, and said nothing.

Garden Primitives

"Cindy's in bed and Mark should be home soon." Her husband was watching the screen again. A log in the fireplace hissed. "Earl," she said, "are you listening?" He swiveled his chair around to face her.

"What, Marilyn?" he flared. "What the hell do you want me to say?" He saw color rush to her cheeks. Her chin began to wobble the way it did before she cried.

"Right," he said, and swiveled away. He could feel her eyes still on him. There was silence and then the den door slammed. He listened to the electric garage door rise, her engine turn over, her wheels back into the driveway, the door sliding down in its track. Quiet. A log in the fireplace popped. Laughter from the idiot box.

THE SCORE IS TIED, sudden death overtime. Lambert passes the puck to Goldy. To Lambert. To Goldy. Across the blue line. The crowd is deafening. It's Goldy to Lambert in front of the net. He shoots, the puck deflects off the post. Lambert retrieves it and circles behind the goal. He turns. He shoots. He scores!!

Mark sank into a snowbank, lay on his back at the far end of the rink. He could see his teammates scramble over the boards. They piled on top of him, gloves scattered on the ice. His family in the VIP box were hugging and cheering; his father looked proud.

Large flakes floated down from the sky. Mark watched them fall out of the blankness. They swirled in the floodlights, landed on his chest, brushed against his

What Mark Couldn't See

nylon jacket. He could see billions of snowflakes. How could they all be different? Tammy had told him so during a storm. She'd been standing at the kitchen window fixing Cindy peanut butter toast. He was surprised she was talking to him; she'd been a total creep for weeks. She'd mope in her room, ignore him completely. When she wasn't ignoring him, she was being mean. Then suddenly she started talking about snowflakes, quiet like she was confiding in him. He stood with her at the kitchen sink and looked out the window at the snow in the yard, lining tree limbs, making hats on bushes, even though he didn't believe her because there was just so much snow not even mentioning places like the North Pole. But there was something about the way she was talking, how she had set down the knife and picked at her fingernail, that caused him to leave it alone, to stand quietly and look out the window with her.

Mark's breath steamed up; the snow fell without a sound. A large flake drifted toward his face. He opened his mouth to catch it on his tongue, but it landed on his eye and melted. His wrist was red–cold where snow had clumped in the gap between his sleeve and glove. The rink lights blinked off and on; the warming house would close in fifteen minutes. The hockey game had ended without his noticing, and he was going to be late getting home.

Garden Primitives

Mark followed the track of his mother's car up the drive. Art class again, he assumed. TV lights flickered across the backyard. He could see his father's chair in the window, the bald spot on the back of his head. The house was warm; it still smelled like pork chops. He quietly, carefully, hung his things in the closet. He took off his boots and tiptoed past the den. "Mark." He was in for it now. He turned the doorknob reluctantly. His father swiveled in his chair. He had a drink in his hand, the photo album open in his lap. His eyes looked tiny and sunk in puffy skin. Mark hardly ever saw him without his glasses on. It made his head seem soft and small. "Do you remember our trip to California?" Mark's father asked, his tiny eyes on him. Mark pushed his hands into his pockets and looked at the floor near his father's feet.

"Sure," he answered. "It was fun."

"I thought so, too," his father murmured, his naked head now turned to the fire. Mark shifted his weight uneasily and waited for his father to say something else. He watched him tilt his glass back, the ice cubes sliding down to his mouth.

"Sorry I'm late," Mark said. "I should have kept better track of the time." But his father kept looking at the fire.

In the girls' room, Cindy was in bed, her eyes closed, her mouth half-open. Her stuffed rabbit had fallen on the floor. Mark put it in bed next to her. His father's

What Mark Couldn't See

puffy face passed through his mind; he'd never seen him look that way before.

Tammy's side of the room was nearly empty. She'd taken all of her cool stuff—her posters, her radio, her hanging bead curtain. She'd left her music box with the twirling ballerina. Her bear, Gregory, was on her bed, patches of fur and bald spots worn smooth. Mark remembered her birthday again.

He left the door to his room open a crack, turned off the light, and jumped into bed. The sheets were cold so he bicycled his legs. He tucked Gregory under his arm but the bear stunk like the baby lotion perfume that Tammy had started wearing by the gallon. Stinky perfume and that baby-blue eye shadow she'd put on in the alley before going to school. The day his father caught her doing it, they screamed so loud he could hear them in the house. Mark was certain that all the neighbors could hear, too. Then his mother, still in her robe, ran out and joined the screaming. He poured Cindy's cereal and crunched his own loudly, trying to drown out the noise, trying to drown out the embarrassment he felt. His father stormed in, purple with anger; his mother followed after him, crying. Tammy didn't come back in. That time she stayed away for three days. Mark thought about his father in the room below him, his tiny eyes, his puffy skin. It was Tammy's fault, the way his dad looked. The bear stunk, and he

Garden Primitives

threw it across the room where it landed facedown by the closet door. They were right about Tammy; she was wrecking everything.

Mark rocked himself back and forth and looked out the window next to his bed. He could see the Masons' house across the street, the long icicles hanging from the eaves. He could see their front yard all covered with snow. The sidewalks were white again, and he could hear someone shoveling. He rocked in time to the rhythmic sound of aluminum scraping over cement. There was a star in the sky, and Mark could see the moon slide in and out between the clouds.

What Mark couldn't see was his sister Tammy, standing by the elm on the Masons' boulevard. Her brown boots with snow-caked laces, her jacket open, no hat, her fingernails bitten down raw. She was watching her house in the dead of winter, the dark windows, the impenetrable front door. He couldn't see the mascara streaked on her cheek as she watched smoke stream up from the chimney, watched it angle in the wind like a gray dog running, secrets clamped tight in its icy white teeth.

What Mark Couldn't See

↣ *Planted*

SUZANNE FELT THE PRESS of her weight, the hard ground against her skull, against the triangular bones of her shoulder blades. She felt it at her hips and heels, round, flattening the grass below. Her feet seemed far-away from her. She tried to let her body settle into the ground which was cool and a little bit damp. The sun was like the pale yellow center of a morning glory, blue petals of sky fanning around it. Its warmth welled in the hollows of her pores, seeped into her shirt, draped over her thighs; it cupped her kneecaps dripping down; she imagined it leaving yellow pools in the grass. Warmth above. Cool below. A breeze stirred the lawn and the fine hair on her arms. It carried the sharp fragrance of chive, planted at the edge of the garden. Suzanne watched the stalks out of the corner of her eye as they swayed, rippling green against each other. Their purple crowns bobbed and wavered in the air.

The warmth of the sun flowed down her insteps. Her feet seemed faraway. One set of toes fell toward her house, the other pointed to the low garden fence. A dancer's stance, the splay of her feet, from all of those years of rigorous training in Madame Covey's studio. Madame Covey, alabaster-still, hands placed on ivory satin, now colorless inside the coffin, the weight of moist earth pressing in from all sides. The dance studio, too, was only a memory. She could still see the light from the high windows, the dust particles floating in gold. She could see the way the light angled down, finally lying in stretched squares across the floor. And the smell that belonged only to that place, leotard sweat and a hint of lavender, of Madame Covey in her black skirt. "From your center, Suzanne," she'd always say, with her fist pressing into her own stomach. "You have the fire, but where is your center?"

An ant crawled up Suzanne's waist along a thin line of exposed flesh. She fought the urge to sweep it away. The trace of its legs tickled her skin. She tried to let the creature be, closing her eyes tight against its movements. An act of courage. Testing herself.

She'd found coarse gray anthills scattered over the garden in late spring when she finally turned the dirt. Standing on the shovel's lip, the metal slicing into the soil. She'd worked methodically though her thoughts arced and churned. The metal sliced down and she lifted the shovel. Brown ants swarmed, their colony unearthed, hidden a spade's depth below the surface. The ants scrambled, bursting out from the center. She, some godzilla in a black-and-white movie. The swarming repulsed her, but she watched transfixed. It was as if she had sheared off the top of her head, the scrambling ants mirroring her own swarming thoughts. She felt exposed though she knew that was crazy. Her thoughts were invisible, hidden from view, hidden in a mass of bone and tissue, circular, contoured, her common head.

The image of the ants last returned to her at a concert, as she listened and watched the musicians' gestures that, when combined, filled the hall with Bach's inner rhythms. Fingers slid along catgut, cheeks rounded with breath, emptied, pushing air through reeds. She listened and watched but her thoughts arced and churned. Before her were rows of heads, circular forms with varying mats of hair, all filled, she imagined, with billions of ants, continuous thoughts, random swarming. If they could be seen, the ants set free, she knew that the hall would be filled entirely. The walls covered; the sleek wood of the cellos, the cords of the microphones that hung from the ceiling, and the people in their clothes all covered, too; not a shoe visible for the thickness of them.

Suzanne squinted against the sun's brightness. Rainbow discs like fish scales formed in her lashes. The sun and the blue petal sky, but the blue was spectral and elusive. Suzanne raised her hand overhead and dragged it slowly across the sky. Blue wedges formed between each finger. The color, the same as Madame Covey's eyes. She could drag her hand through the blue air and bring it back to her face, colorless.

The last time she had gone to visit, she found Madame Covey in her wheelchair, her face half-slack from multiple strokes. Her body was like a feather, weightless, resting to one side. She hadn't acknowledged Suzanne's presence. She did not seem to hear the music she'd brought. Her eyes were vacant and dusty, reflecting Suzanne's image when she tried to see in. But then Madame Covey's hand was in motion, beating a vague rhythm against the wheelchair. And Suzanne, searching in Madame Covey's eyes, thought she'd caught a glimpse of her, a swatch of black skirt at the end of a hallway that disappeared through a door.

Something poked the back of her knee. A blade of grass or perhaps a bug. She jiggled her leg at the tiny intrusion and turned her head, flattening her cheek to the ground. She closed one eye against the sun and found the grass suddenly unfamiliar. The lawn was a wildwood of shades of green, cypress, chartreuse. Lines creased down the center. An insect's universe, she thought, taking in the foreign terrain. Some blades stood erect, some leaned forming triangles. Gold withered blades curled on the dirt. But, she thought, through a faceted eye, the lines would all tumble, kaleidoscope, merging at every conceivable angle. And the bugs on their wire legs would pick paths over and under the blades. To what end? Maybe the compost pile where just this morning she had dumped a plate of onion skins, melon rind, coffee grounds, and the slimy stems of peonies from the vase on her bookshelf.

The white balls of petals had perfumed the air, even as they fell away. They landed on the shelf and on the wooden floor where they scattered in a loose arc. She'd swept around them, liking them there, as beautiful fallen as on the stem. But they began to soften, to curl and brown along their creases. The water in the vase turned green, reflected green against the white wall. So she'd swept the petals into a dustpan. The water reeked, vile, down the drain. She held her breath, filled the vase quickly with dish soap, overpowered by the stench of it. Strangely, the compost pile didn't smell. There she dumped the remnants of her diet, knocking the plate against the wooden bin. Banana peels mixed with garden weeds, shriveling, rotting, pressing down, turning into mulch with time, all of the volume going out of things. And the ants foraging through the tangle of green to drag away a piece of orange, flies licking at old red beans.

A cool crept over Suzanne's cheeks and the orange light through her eyelids went gray. Above her were clouds, not a heavy flatness, but a gathering of forms, airy, floating. A phone wire bisected her view and the clouds moved toward it like a finishing line. One cloud had the shape of a turtle, another a bird, or perhaps an angel, the kind one could make lying in snow or sand. She watched the clouds draw near the wire though she knew there would be no surprise at the finish, no cloud would sprint up from behind. The strange herd advanced in sync, as if resting on a huge glass platter that flattened their bottoms and turned them gray.

Suzanne could see her place at the barre in Madame Covey's studio. Near her reflection was a long dark line formed by the meeting of two mirrors. That line, she thought, she must have been about ten. At the barre, practicing grace, her arm floating down from over her head, slightly arced, her hand held just so. She was learning to defy gravity, to make her arm appear as weightless as the dust that lingered in the high window light. As her arm came down, her fingers neared the line. She had been obsessed by it. She'd watch her fingers float down in the glass, approaching the line like some unknown territory, and part of her wanted to lean over and touch it. It excited her but it was scary, too, like daring to swim under the dock at the cabin where the water was shaded and unfriendly. Her bones lengthened, her legs grew, and her arms elongated, rounded with muscle. Suzanne forgot about the line entirely until one day, as her arm floated down and she felt as light as the swirling dust, she noticed the line where the two mirrors met, her hand held just so on the other side, sliced above the wrist like a mannequin's. She'd felt no triumph, no mystery solved, just a bland acknowledgement of her own silliness and bafflement at the passage of time.

Her phone was ringing. She could hear its measured chirp through the upstairs window, hear her own garbled voice, a long beep, then another voice indiscernible. She wouldn't go answer. She did not want to move. The platter of clouds slid on overhead. It had been a year since she'd visited Madame Covey. The plane angled up through heavy gray. Pressure held her shoulders to the seat. She remembered the wing, stiff, undaunted, slicing through the misty darkness, lightening, thinning, gray like smoke, the sharp glint of sun as it hit the metal, the breakthrough to another world. White swells formed far-off buttes that shone against a brilliant blue. And the sun hung in its prescribed place despite what she had perceived on the ground with the taxi meter clicking, the slap of the windshield wipers, water beads streaming up toward the roof.

The cloud tops beckoned like a thousand thrones and she was free to wander from perch to perch, to bound in great leaps, trampoline, to rest, lying cushioned in the billowing white. It was silent there, silent and warm. The only intrusion, the plane's rippling shadow.

Planted

Suzanne watched the mouth of a dragon-shaped cloud. Its jaw thinned, dissipated, curled out of existence. The clouds had passed the telephone wire. The angel had lost one of its wings. She hadn't noticed which cloud had touched first though she had been looking at them all along.

The sun was hot. Suzanne peeled back her shirt to feel the heat penetrate her stomach. She had meant to make herself some breakfast, but there were fruit flies floating around the compost plate. She'd come down to the yard to empty it. She'd knocked the plate against the wooden bin and wandered into her neglected garden. She'd squatted next to the pepper plants. The soles of her feet pressed into the dirt. She'd pushed back the leaves in the row of radishes, their prickly undersides nicking her hand. And she had been startled to see them there, their firm red shoulders embedded in the dirt, though it was she who had planted the beige nuggets of seed. She had seen the pale green line of the seedlings. She'd noticed that the leaves had broadened. But the radish itself that had grown underground was an alchemy she could not comprehend. She took hold of one and pulled it from the soil. It came round and hard-red, clumped with dirt. Below it, a single hairy root.

There was still dirt on her fingers and streaked on her side where she had scratched at the ant. The plate of radishes was near her in the grass, green-plumed crimson balls, pulled from the incubating darkness where small thin roots pointed down, fringing the top of the frame in her mind. And there would be longer, thicker ones, the roots of shrubs, her tomato plants. And the massive branching roots of trees spreading out and down, snaked around rock, down past her house's foundation. Between the roots, blackness, like a photo negative, yet solid, everything having mass. Except where dull-eyed animals burrowed there would be space, cylindrical tunnels, tubes of air where one's fingers could wiggle. Suzanne tried to imagine down farther through the bedrock's vast mantle of stone but her thoughts were like a puny shovel striking against the mantle's hardness.

A screen door slammed. Casey, her neighbor's labrador, appeared. Suzanne stretched her arms overhead, gently working the muscles along her back. Her rib cage rose, her bones defined in arcs that pushed up against her skin. The dog sniffed at her head and the plate of radishes, then walked off to his spot under the picnic table. The sun striped his fur yellow down through the table planks. Suzanne raised her foot toward the sky and turned her ankle around in a circle, changed direction, circled again. She pulled her leg flat to her chest, felt the muscle stretch down through her buttock. Her calf where she held it was rough against her fingers, dented from pressing into the grass. The same routine for the other leg: circling ankle, the deep pull of muscle, then still once again, she lay in the grass. Still except for her murmuring stomach. Potatoes were frying in somebody's kitchen. The smell of their browning wafted over the fence. She was hungry but she felt fastened to the earth, pinned down like a butterfly in a chloroform daze.

From light-years away the sun's fire touched her. She was lost in the ash-orange shimmering of her eyelids, the embers glowing through thin flaps of skin. In her mind, she pushed up past the clouds, through blue and more blue, beyond the petals that kept her from seeing the thick of space. There, breath would be impossible, in the silent, chilly company of stars, the sun the central force of nine spinning planets, circling like dancers around its fire.

Her thoughts were a puny shovel striking the stones' hardness, mantles of bedrock buried below her. But she knew there was water, water that moved. She imagined it creeping in black streams like crude oil, pooled in lakes, black mirrors without reflection, where no weed swayed, no fin sliced the surface. The miles of rock where no creature dwelled. The rock growing too hot to touch, melting, molten viscosity, the black-flame center of buried heat.

There was fire below her, there was fire above. And Suzanne lay between them in the grass. "From your center." She heard the words, saw the fist pushing against the black skirt. The dog sank down in the grass alongside her. His fur was hot against her skin, and their bodies pushed at each other with breath. The plate of radishes lay in the grass, two small brown ants traversing their roundness.

→ *There Are No Green Butterflies*

THEY SIT IN THE SAND out of reach of each other. It is a windless Sunday afternoon, late fall, and the trees on the riverbank are mostly bare.

She turns her head and looks at his profile. The brim of his hat lines a shadow across his cheek. His nose is sturdy, his gaze, distant. Like that of an explorer, she thinks. If she had her camera, she'd use it. She would try to capture the shadow in his eyes, in hope of understanding him.

"What?" he says, in that slow tone of his, the word more invitation than question.

"I'm just looking at you."

The sexual attraction is so strong, she can feel it, she thinks, vibrating between them. She wants to kiss him, but doesn't. Instead she scrapes a trench in the sand with the heel of her shoe.

Crows caw from the top of an oak. Their black wings flap as they posture, shift weight. She is unsure how to begin. She looks at his hands, his blunt fingers.

She'd been amazed at the agility of his fingers spidering over the neck of his battered guitar.

"This piece isn't finished," he'd said the first time he'd played for her.

"The ending made me see water. Thin water going over stone."

"You would," he'd smiled.

She is dragging her hand back and forth in the sand forming a miniature esker under her palm. She should just blurt it out, say, you're driving me crazy.

"Lots of people need their pianos moved this week?" she asks.

He nods and shrugs. "Business is steady."

She calculates the weeks they've been seeing each other. Five. She's dying to sleep with him. It seems impossible that it hasn't happened. They are leaves that won't fall from a tree. She sees them bright and dangling, always on the verge of a twirling dance in the wind. Why does she continue to wait for him, to take a chance, to let herself be vulnerable when half of the time she ends up feeling bad?

Gravity is bigger than both of them, she thinks. It's the inevitability of the leaves. She can be patient. She has plenty of work to do. Her darkroom is full of film, portraits of people waiting at bus stops. She straightens her legs out in front of her and knocks her sandy tennis shoes together.

"There are no green butterflies," he states, looking straight ahead at the brown water of the Mississippi. He says this solemnly as if this fact contains all the world's mystery and all its disappointment.

She tries to recall if she has ever seen a green butterfly, in a meadow, or on a specimen plaque, not that she has any reason to disbelieve him. She loves this about him, the odd facts he tells her. She hoards them, threads them like glass beads on a string.

"It fascinates me. Before I die, I want to have a theory about it. Why wouldn't there be green butterflies?"

She smiles because this fascinates him. She makes figure-eights in the sand, picturing him old among specimen drawers.

"They're like flowers," he continues.

She agrees, thinking of butterflies like petals, translucent strokes of color against a blue sky.

"They do the same things, but in separate stages. Seeds are like cocoons. The plant is the caterpillar. The flower, like the butterfly, is a reproductive stage . . ."

Always back to reproduction, she thinks. Is this supposed to be some kind of torture? The mating habits of Eskimos, of chimpanzees, of young city kids . . . in one form or another, he's always talking about it. Not that it's bad. She likes his frankness, how he says the word *penis* as easily as *pancake*. Maybe it's lust that causes her to hear sex in everything he says.

There Are No Green Butterflies

". . . Moths, too. They live solely to reproduce. A female luna moth doesn't even have a mouth. She'll live maybe ten days or so, staying in a relatively small area. She waits for the males to come to her."

"Luna moths don't have mouths?" Another glass bead for her collection.

"They're the most ethereally beautiful things I've ever seen." She notices how his eyes soften as he talks. "They are swallow-tailed, with furry white bodies . . ." She watches him fade into a night forest where the large moth pulses on the trunk of a tree.

"Their wings are the most miraculous color, a blue-green, but soft, indescribable. There's a red stripe at the top of the wing and a gold line . . . I'm lecturing again, aren't I?"

She appreciates that he recognizes this. Usually, she's interested. His passionate focus on the natural world allows her to see in new ways. But lately, she finds herself drifting. Frustrated. When his eyes are on butterflies, they can't see her.

A woodpecker's hollow knock repeats in the woods. "So," she says, to claim the space before he starts telling her all about woodpeckers. He turns and the electricity arcs. He smiles as if he can feel it too, but then looks away.

She erases her eights with the flat of her hand, and starts digging her fingers in randomly.

Garden Primitives

He lights his pipe, sucking the match flame into the bowl.

She tries to arrange the words in her mind, to be kind, not confrontational.

"I don't know what to make of you," is all that comes out. "I don't understand what you want from me."

He nods slowly as if he has heard this before. This gives her pause. It is not a good sign. A beer can is floating in the river and they both watch it idle by. It bobs, changes its tilt with the current.

He speaks, without looking at her. "I'm not used to being with someone like you."

Her hand stops digging in the sand. "How so?"

"You're glamorous," he accuses.

She sees magazine models with long thin thighs, then laughs as she looks at her baggy jeans. She fans her fingers displaying short nails.

"Are you referring to the way I dress, or just in general my statuesque presence?"

He lowers his head and fingers the rim of his hat. He is amused, but he's not laughing.

She waits. Glamorous?

"At the concert the other night . . . I'm not used to being with the prettiest girl in the room."

She is pleased to hear how he'd felt. The "girl" surprises her, but she lets it pass. It sounds sweet in an innocent way.

There Are No Green Butterflies

That night she had dressed for him, wanting to look good but not like she was trying. A casual, sexy look, she'd thought. She could feel his eyes take her in when she opened the door. She could feel him behind her as they climbed the stairs. In the kitchen, she stood at the counter chopping an onion. He sat in a chair, watching her, the energy flying back and forth between them, making her feel so self-conscious that it was like she'd never cut an onion before.

"Hey, we're lucky, you and I," she'd told him, remembering that they'd won five dollars from the lottery ticket he'd left on her windshield.

"I'm starting to like this feeling lucky," he'd said.

After the concert they went out for a drink, then sat in his car in front of her house. She wanted to touch him, but stopped herself having vowed not to initiate again. The energy was impossible to ignore, like magnets held close, circling. But he started talking about the Bering Strait and the lifestyles of early nomadic people.

"They traveled on foot, the men hunting together. Often they had multiple sexual partners, which makes more sense when you think about evolution."

He talked for a good half hour, as she tried to read between the lines, to observe his face in the dim light. So much for the clean sheets on the bed, she'd thought.

That night, like others, she'd decided to stop seeing him. She'd lain in bed exacerbated. How were they supposed to discover what was possible if he wouldn't let things flow? But sooner or later she'd turn on herself with the fine-edged knife of self-blame. Stop being so impatient. Give him room. He'll come around when he's ready.

A riverboat pushing two empty barges maneuvers upstream between red and green buoys.

Okay, he thinks she's pretty. It's nice that he said so, but it doesn't clarify the picture any.

"So . . . this is a problem . . . because what? . . . you only date ugly women?" She says this jokingly, but he is thinking it over.

The wake of the barge pushes against the bank, rocking a dead tree lodged in the shallows.

"It's more than that," he says. "Your life seems so together."

She can't imagine what he sees when he looks at her.

"I don't think that our lives are so different. I have my camera and you have your guitar. Waiting tables is awfully glamorous. And it's got to be about as spiritually fulfilling as moving pianos." She stops, feeling the utter absurdity. Against what is she defending herself?

He laughs.

"I suppose that I'm less of a loner than you," she says, "And okay, I admit it. I own more than two forks."

He gives her leg a little shove, but then his face drops into seriousness.

There Are No Green Butterflies

"So, this is the thing. If I were destitute, and less attractive, there wouldn't be any problem?"

"I need to feel useful," he says.

"I can think of a few ways you could be of use."

He smiles.

"Everyone wants to feel useful," she says.

He knocks his pipe against his shoe. "It means a lot to me."

"Like filling my tires and buying me that tire gauge? That was very thoughtful." She places her hand on his shoulder for a moment, but it doesn't move into her or respond in any way. "Fine, I can make a list. For starters, my bathroom window needs rehanging."

He snorts.

"So what? You want my life to be a mess?" She can't believe that this is what he means.

He takes off his hat and runs his hand over his head. "I think that your feelings are stronger than mine."

She lights a cigarette and puts the match in the sand, takes a long drag and blows out the smoke, watches it blend into the pale sky.

"No problem with your ego, anyway."

"I will fail," he says, and throws a stone into the water. "I can't give you what you want."

"What I want? You presume to know?"

"Look. Say in a couple of years you need to move for a job or something. I don't think I could do it. I'm

Garden Primitives

not good at it."

"In a couple of years? Jesus. How in the world did you get to two years from now? Shit, I haven't even bought new underwear yet," she lies.

He looks shocked for a moment, and then he grins.

"Do women really do that?" he asks.

A dog is running on the opposite bank, barking at its owner to throw a stick. She balls up, wrapping her arms around her legs. She feels like she has stepped off some dizzying ride and can't tell what's spinning, her brain or the ground.

"I don't even know what I want with you," she says, attempting to allay his fears. "One minute you're close and then, boom." She gestures to the other side of the river. "You might as well be over there. I feel like we have potential, but it's pretty hard to figure anything out when you're miles away half the time."

"I'm sorry," he says, and he sounds like he means it.

What she has said is true. Not entirely. She knows that she wants him. She has since their second date.

They were on their way to a state park to hike.

"Do you mind if we stop first?" he'd asked. "It won't take long. I've just got to fit some casters on a piano."

She followed him into a retirement home, past the office, and into the living room where a tiny woman was parked on the sofa. Her face was interesting, old and childlike at once. He laid his hat on top of the baby grand, then crawled underneath it. She watched as he positioned himself on all fours near one of the piano legs. He arched his back and lifted the piano. With one hand he fitted the caster.

She caught a glimpse of herself in the wall mirror grinning like an idiot at his Herculean feat. The old woman on the couch was smiling as well.

"These aren't right," he said. "They're a hair too small. I'm going to need some tape and scissors. Sorry, I thought this would be really quick."

"Thanks," he said softly every time she handed him a length of tape. She liked how it felt to do a project with him even though he was doing all the hard work. With her roll of tape, she knelt on the floor and watched as he positioned himself by the third leg. She looked at his butt, his legs spread. She watched as he arched his back and she felt the urge to lie right down under him.

The dog is swimming in the water with a stick, angling toward the shore against the current. It climbs out and shakes rings of water from its coat. She lights another cigarette.

"Look," she says, and then hesitates. She's not sure she wants to tell him this; she finds it embarrassing to admit to herself. "Before I met you I was feeling lonely. I started to ask . . . well . . . I don't know who, the universe I guess, to send me someone."

Garden Primitives

He doesn't scoff or laugh at this.

"I don't meet men I'm attracted to very often. So maybe that's why my feelings seem so strong to you."

"I've never been the answer to somebody's prayer before."

She blows smoke sharply to the sky.

"Did I say you were?"

Smiling, he fixes his eyes steadily on hers, for a second, just long enough for a pulsing exchange of energy.

A bumblebee hovers around her leg and she fights the urge to shoo it away. She is trying to be more generous around bugs, to discover what he finds so fascinating. They watch it light on a stalk of goldenrod and nuzzle its head into a blossom.

"They'll sleep overnight if the temperature drops," he says. "It has to be warm for their muscles to work. That's why they're furry. It's insulation."

"A nice way to wake up, with your head in a flower." She wishes she hadn't said this. She might as well have just taken off her clothes and stepped naked and uninvited into his bed.

"They specialize in particular flowers," he says. "Some go to goldenrod, some petunias. Each type of flower requires a strategy, different behaviors to get to the pollen . . ." He is off. She envisions the close-ups she'd taken of monarchs on one of their day-long hikes together. Stupid. Faces are what fascinate her.

There Are No Green Butterflies

The Hmong woman waiting for the twenty-two bus. She'd caught an elusive anger in her eyes.

A clank and rattling issues from the woods and a train engine rolls onto the railroad bridge. Pigeons take flight from the iron trestle, fanning out in the gray sky. She looks at his face in the grainy light. All their talk is a dance around the one thing she knows. Okay, just name it, she thinks.

"There's this huge attraction," she begins, her hand defining the space between them. "It's fierce. You do feel it, right?"

He nods his head slowly in affirmation as a sound comes rumbling from deep in his chest. It sounds like sex. It sounds like it pains him.

"Right," she says, and lets out a long breath. She knew it. She knew it was mutual.

"Sex is holy," he says, looking off in the distance.

This slays her. It makes her want him even more. But wait, this from the man who quotes Darwin, who talks about sex like most people talk about weather? She is trying to make sense of his contradictions. There's a picture that she can't compose, the elements fight each other, they refuse to line up. Something sickly familiar turns in her stomach. Hadn't she learned long ago to recognize the difference between what she sees and what is?

He takes off his hat and lets it dangle between his legs. For a long time they are silent.

"What? What are you thinking about?" she asks.

"Bees," he says.

She wishes she hadn't called him that morning, that they hadn't talked about any of it.

"I should go," she says quietly.

He looks startled.

"What am I supposed to do, convince you?" she says.

"That's not it."

"Is there someone else?"

"Not exactly."

"Damn it. You don't make any sense."

He nods, but he doesn't speak. He just stares imperviously ahead at the river water flowing southward. She feels tears stinging behind her eyes. She should get up and walk away, but she can't force herself to do it.

She sees them as they'd been a few weeks earlier, a perfect day to be on the water. Her paddle dipping into the reflection of fall trees.

"Do you want to keep going?" he'd asked.

She'd just pointed her paddle downstream and nodded.

"Girl after my own heart," he'd said.

Two young boys are walking at the river's edge carrying fishing poles and tackle.

"This is all wrong," she says when they've passed.

She places her hand on his shoulder, and he turns. She pushes to her knees and goes to him, straddling herself

There Are No Green Butterflies

across his lap. She takes his face in her hands and kisses him. His lips welcome hers, but it's not long before they stiffen. She pulls away and looks into his eyes.

"Damn you," she says, and tries to get up, but he's holding her down by her shoulders. She bats his arms away and stands. "What is your problem? You're making me nuts."

"Maybe we shouldn't see each other anymore," he says.

"But that's stupid. You haven't given it a chance. We haven't even had time to try."

"We haven't had time to make each other miserable."

"We haven't had time to make each other ecstatic."

He shakes his head and picks up his hat, smoothing the brim where she'd knelt on it.

"You're so intense," he accuses.

She nabs the hat out of his hand and throws it like a frisbee across the sand.

"So what if I am? Are you scared of me?"

He stands, wipes the sand from his pants, and walks calmly toward his hat. She kicks sand in his wake, but he doesn't break stride. She wants him to turn around and kick back, she wants to have a screaming fight, a frantic cathartic crying thing that would clear the way so they could start over, new as the curve of the smallest crescent moon.

"You don't make any sense," she yells.

He picks up his hat and faces her. Anger pulses at his temples.

She wants it all back. Every single thing. Every day spent waiting for him to figure it out, every patience, every kind word, every compliment, touch, fantasy; she wants back each and every kiss.

"I'm leaving," he says evenly.

"I guess you are."

And he walks away.

She throws everything she can into the river. Sticks, but they're not heavy enough. Rocks, big ones. She sits and cries.

WITH SHAKING HANDS, she holds a match to her cigarette. The dog and its owner have left. There is only the river and the big black crows. She tells herself she'll be better off in the long run. Does she really want someone who's such a mess? Someone who can't even decipher himself? She's better off. It's his loss.

She looks over her shoulder, but he's nowhere in sight. She remembers the night they climbed over the river on the catwalk beneath the railroad bridge. Glamorous. Intense. "I woke up feeling so happy today," his voice said on her message machine. "Is there someone else?" "Not exactly." His hands on her hips. Two dangling leaves.

The thin knife of self-blame is back in her hand. If she'd been more patient, been more herself. Why does

There Are No Green Butterflies

she always have to push things? She feels hot slices over her skin, feels the knife's stinging edge against her shoulder blade. Yes, there. The smooth surface, her wing-less back.

→ *Submersion*

JOAN STIRRED IN HER BED, groggy from the medication that the doctor and Gloria, the hotel keeper, convinced her to take. She tried to force herself awake, but her eyelids were heavy and kept falling shut. There was the faint sound of singing. Sweet. Melodic. But she wasn't sure if it was real. Her attention strayed around the room, her eyes rolling slowly over the cement walls painted blue like the bottom of a swimming pool. She stared at the shelves and the blue, blue ceiling. Then she discovered the vacant twin bed that lay parallel to hers along the wall. She was dizzy as she started from her bed, driven by the knowledge that she had to get out.

Dusk was falling over Puerto Angel. She had no idea how long she'd been inside, one day or two, possibly a week. She looked out from the balcony in search of some clue, but everything in the village looked unchanged. In the bay, wooden fishing boats aligned themselves with the wind. They tugged at their anchors and rolled in the waves. A kelp-scented breeze pushed the hair from her forehead, and she could taste the air-borne salt on her lips. Her thoughts came in snapshots: the uniformed official from the town of Pochutla; the doctor whose ears seemed too small for his head; and Gloria's face, round and flat, drifting over her bed armed with bowls and hot spoons. Flashing on the water, angry and gray, she felt a wave of nausea rush through her body. She sank down in a chair and held her head in her hands. Something had happened, she wasn't sure what. Her mind was dull and her body numb.

A three-legged starfish and a collection of shells were arranged in the corner of the balcony floor. Joan watched them, eyed their shapes. She pulled a strand of hair from the nape of her neck and ran it repeatedly through her fingers. The urge to return them rose inside her, and she knew that she had to go back to the beach.

She wrapped each shell with measured movements, each one inside of a striped sock, then placed them all snugly into a pack. She tiptoed down the stairs and past the door where Gloria lived with her husband and four polite children. She could hear their television and the clink of dinner dishes. Below the hotel, the town's lights blinked, awaiting the tourists who would come for dinner. Joan crept down the steep hotel steps and walked to the main road that lead out of town.

A group of boys, just finished playing basketball, sat on a stone wall bordering the court. She could feel their eyes on her. No, don't look at them. They watched her pass, talking among themselves, but she kept on going as if none of them existed. She was relieved that the hotel was near the edge of town. Soon she would be alone.

The road wound through a parched landscape that connected the fishing village of Puerto Angel to Poch-utla, a small city with the area's main market. Hills rose on either side of the road, sparse and dusty, scattered with wiry trees. She walked unsteadily as the road climbed and curved, leaving the lights of the town behind. There was no wind, no cicadas or whining traffic, just the sound of her footsteps and a barking dog.

Around the next bend there would be a shack. She remembered having passed it before. It was a scant building with a corrugated tin roof and a large open patio with hammocks and chickens. She could hear a radio as she approached, Spanish words rising and fall-ing over static. The smell of fried fish drifted down the hillside. There were hammocks stretched wide and weighted with people.

Joan felt gutted, scraped to the rind. She considered leaving the road for the hills. She could climb into their darkness, find a spot in the dirt, turn off her flashlight, and disappear. If it weren't for the shells that she carried on her back she could. Yes. Just dissolve.

The moon rose in the eastern sky. Nearly full and eggshell white, its light washed out the night's new stars. Joan watched it ascend, she picked out its face. The same face she'd known as a child, high in the Wisconsin sky. She'd sing to it when she couldn't get to sleep, and now, again, its presence was comforting. Loyal moon finding her on that foreign road. And as it rose, its light brightened. The hills took on the gray-black of etchings, and she could see the silhouette of the dump.

The dump looked different than she remembered so she had to search for the path with her flashlight. As she walked between the piles of junk, her skin began to tingle and her breath grew shallow. Something moved over one of the mounds, causing a tin can to roll onto the path. Then she heard it. It was neither animal nor human, but garbled as if coming through water, not air. She was too scared to move either forward or back, but the noise in her ears made staying impossible.

Joan bolted into the woods, the shells bouncing against her spine as she stumbled over roots that criss-crossed the path. She didn't stop until she reached the cliff. She stood panting and crying and sucking in air. The water stretched out like black onyx below her; the white lines of the surf unrolled on the sand. She hadn't been followed; the path was empty. She stumbled down the switchback to the beach.

She tried to stay out of reach of the salty tongues of water, as she unwrapped each shell and held it out. When the water came up, she gave the shell back. The water took it tumbling down the slope of sand, making a sound like clicking teeth. (95

She felt calm as she gathered the scattered socks, matching them by the color of their stripes, balling them into pairs as she'd done so often. The socks, yes. She'd give them back, too. She cast the cloth balls into the surf. Never in her life had an act seemed so meaningful, and this realization brought her to a halt. She looked around the deserted beach and wondered what she was doing there. She thought about finding the doctor in town. He had spoken to her in English and his eyes were kind.

Joan sensed movement at the edge of her vision, something at the far end of the cove. It looked like a boulder inching out of the surf. She closed her eyes, then looked again. She sighted it against another rock and watched the distance grow between them. It was moving slow and steady toward the back of the beach. Joan moved toward it at an intersecting angle. Stopping when it stopped, she mirrored its movements. When she got close she could hear its labored breathing, see it lift itself up on its broad front flippers, then shove its weight forward with its powerful rears. It looked as if it had crawled out of the past, out of a time before people, as old as stone.

The turtle stopped where the sand gave way to scrub, not far from a listing palapa. It sat still for a moment then disappeared behind a noisy shower of sand. Joan crawled around the hut for a better view. The turtle looked like it was trying to swim, all of its flippers in motion at once, throwing the sand in high arcs. It stopped when the pit was as big as its body, then it raised up on its front flippers and started digging with its back. It stared straight ahead, seeming lost in thought, its body moving methodically.

Joan dug too, pushing sand from around where she knelt.

With its rear flippers to either side of the hole, the turtle squirted mucus into the pit. A tear carved a path down its sandy face while its eggs dropped away, disappearing below.

When the last eggs had fallen, the turtle came to. She seemed surprised at her surroundings, like a sleepwalker awakening in another room. She froze as if sensing danger, then filled the hole with renewed energy. Pushing sand over the eggs, packing it down with her weight, she turned in circles, scooped and tamped, working like time might run out. When the nest was concealed, she turned back to the sea, and with the same graceless movements, she shoved herself forward. Her body left a wide track in the sand. Joan crawled after her, shocked she was leaving. She rose up on her knees, her hands hanging helpless, feeling like a baby had been left on her doorstep. She watched as her shell bobbed in the breakers, . . . once, . . . twice, and then she was gone.

THE SUN IS BIG AND PINK and distorted and close to touching the water on the horizon. Joan steps out of the palapa, where she's lived for eight weeks, and shields her eyes from the slanting light. She's been edgy for days and her sleep has been poor. She surveys the steep angled cliffs around her cove. They hold rock and scrub trees; hawks launch from their tops. A light-haired dog has taken up residence there. She feels it watching her from behind boulders and trees, feels its presence even when she can't see it. Each day it seems to push closer.

She checks the nest. It's undisturbed. The cove is deserted this evening, as usual. Local people come occasionally, but they stick to the other side of the beach near the path that leads out, and where the palm trees offer shade. She walks the crescent of oatmeal-white sand to the spit of rock that forms one arm of her cove. No sign of the turtle once again. The rocks are still filled with afternoon heat; they sting the backs of her legs when she sits. She positions herself on her usual ledge, her feet resting on the rock shelf below. Joan wakes each day in time to witness the transformation. Her internal clock is turned upside down. It has adapted to the rhythm of her nocturnal life.

Joan doesn't trust the sea, not by day. Its jade-colored water shimmers like cut crystal and its cool breezes lure, promise relief from the sun. Only at night is it true to itself. Oily black, it cloaks pale creatures who feed on each other in a frenzy of instinct.

The pink sun dips into the sea and dissolves over the surface in a line that points toward her. She concentrates on the water below. Sunset, she'd discovered, is a con, a grand distraction to keep one's eyes upturned as the true nature of the sea reveals itself below. She herself had been fooled and had stood among the tourists who oohed and aahed from the safety of their balconies in town. But that seems like another life. The turtle nest is everything now.

It's the dog again, she can hear it barking. She jumps boulders back to the sand, but she can't spot it on the bluff. The last of the light lingers in the sky, turning the water silver-pink as it slides in semicircles over the sand. The ghost crabs appear as she walks back toward her hut, zipping sideways in front of her. Their fist-sized bodies dot the beach with shells luminescent, the color of bone. They freeze when she approaches, or pop down a hole, only to appear again as if testing her. Joan scans the hills, looking for the dog, then turns back to her hut, cutting her walk short.

She picks up a plastic bottle and a milky piece of glass which she'll add to the pile of things she has collected. Near her hut in the pastel light, she can see the blue snorkeling flipper perched on a stick. It stands like a flag over the pile of debris.

Her hut is lit with votive candles in order to spare flashlight batteries. Their flames bounce her shadow around, rippling it over the stick walls. Her bed is a beach blanket along the wall. Near it, a small suitcase lies in the sand. She uses it as a bedside table. It is covered with candles and wax flows obscuring the skateboarding stickers adhered to its side. She uses her own suitcase, which lies in the center of the floor as a table and work space. A rope suspends her backpack from the thatched roof. She unknots it and the pack lowers. She learned to hang her food after her first encounter with the ants. She eats the orange and saves the crackers for the road. Over the last month her appetite has come back, forcing her to make regular trips to town.

She puts on her dirty red windbreaker and smooths her hair into a ponytail. She hears a sound, hushed like breathing. She stands still to listen, but then it is gone. With the dull tip of a boy scout knife, she pokes a new hole in the flesh of her belt. Her body has changed, shrunk and hardened. It no longer reflects its thirty-eight years, its thirteen years working a desk job at the college, its bearing a son, its general preference for food over exercise. Joan has no pride in her new appearance, though she likes the feel of the cliffs of her hip bones and the plateau of her belly when she lies on her back. The little grooming she does is for the townspeople. She knows they stare at her when she walks by, and that they whisper about her behind their hands. There are times when she wants to make them understand, but she can't explain what she has no words for herself, and she can't risk exposing the existence of the nest. She fits the large pack on her back, then fumbles with the straps of the small, neon-green one that she wears across her chest to carry water. She blows out the candles one by one.

It's quiet and the early evening stars are out. At first, they had seemed random to her, a spattering of light strewn across the darkness. Now she recognizes patterns and knows their journeys as they move across the night sky. There's a kite, a snake, the horns of a bull.

Joan climbs the switchback out of the cove. No dog. No people. Still, the nest lies unguarded. She had laid dried palm fronds over the nest and circled it with locks of her hair to form a human-scented moat that would ward off predators. If she could stop her body's demand for food, she would never leave the nest alone. There are too many dangers and there have been threats.

She had been sleeping fitfully. The heat was so strong that, even in her shelter, her body felt like suet, boneless and soft. She heard voices outside, too close to her hut. Within seconds she was standing out in the sun; her face was slack and creased from her beach towel. Two old women were nearing the nest. They were walking the scrub line hunting for eggs. Carrying long sticks, they would push them down deep, then pull them back out and examine their ends. Joan grabbed a plastic bottle from her mound. She hurled it, hitting one of them in the back. They turned in unison, stunned and angry. She threw another that landed in a bush. The two held hands and scurried away. They tossed back angry Spanish words. Joan stood like a warrior armed with garbage.

It's hunger forcing her to leave. She turns inland and follows the circle of her flashlight, which jitters along in the dry dirt. Crooked trees grow out of the tangle of underbrush, flank her on either side of the path. It is warmer in the woods and startlingly quiet. The absence of the sound of the surf alarms her, though on the beach she hardly hears it anymore. She holds tight to the flashlight, moves it from side to side, scanning a large area of ground. Twice she hears a snap in the woods, but she doesn't shine her light toward the noise for fear it will meet with the dog's shining eyes.

The path before her threads through debris—broken cement blocks, rusty scrap metal, and an abandoned orange car with a busted-out windshield—before climbing a rise to the two-lane road. She has made it through the dump many times without incident. Even so, like a child passing a graveyard, she holds her breath and runs for the road. She forces herself to remember the garbled sound, as if holding it in her thoughts will keep her from hearing it.

On the road, she stops to adjust the chest pack; its weightless straps keep sliding down her shoulders. She hears a bus downshift, sees its lights on the road. It slows as it nears, but she waves it past. She smells its exhaust, watches its red taillights until they disappear around a bend. She has no intention of boarding the bus with its harsh electricity and riders who will stare. The fabric of her windbreaker swishes as she walks. It sounds so loud in her ears that she has to keep turning, checking to be sure that she is alone. Her stomach growls, and she takes out the crackers. She'll think about the turtle—not worry about the dog—how it turned away and went back to the sea. What did it feel? she wonders, did it feel at all? Maybe she had left heavy with regret, knowing she couldn't survive if she stayed. Maybe she carried this truth and this pain like an added weight on her broad humped back. Joan sees the turtle digging its nest, robotically shifting the sand with its flippers. She wonders whether it had to think about its movements or if its actions were just a reflex, the same as a swallow or a blink. And then its watery eyes and its trance when the eggs fell away. Perhaps the trance was a

Garden Primitives

trick of nature to keep her laying even if danger were near. Or maybe it was a trance of communion, and the tears an expression of both greeting and farewell.

She crumples the wrapper and puts it in her pocket, hoping that the turtle has stayed near. That it swims just offshore, waiting for its young to come into the water. She needs to believe the turtle cares. It makes her feel that she's not alone, that she shares the responsibility for this long gestation. To think otherwise overwhelms her with sadness, for the turtle, the eggs, for any species controlled by the oblivious acts of instinct.

The lights of the village lie below her. They form a bright band where the town hugs the shore, then thin to white dots up in the hills. At one time, Joan had loved the town. Now it was an obstacle she had to take on. She used to walk through the streets with her senses wide open, taking in what she could of the culture around her. She would gather and sift, assume and postulate, try to draw parallels to her own life. She was like a snorkeler who floated over land, fascinated and eager, yet always aware of the sensation that she was on the outside looking in.

Joan hears a crunch in the gravel behind her, a rustle in the bushes alongside the road, then the rhythmic panting of the light-haired dog. The hairs rise on the back of her neck, and she bounds down the hill letting gravity have its way.

The south end of town is empty. The post office and fishing cooperative are locked and dark, and the construction site looks hollow and eerie. A group of teenage girls are gathered by the basketball court. Their talk is marked with laughter and poses and preening tosses of shiny black hair. They pay no attention to Joan as she passes. A couple strolls toward her, hand in hand. Their faces are flushed from a day in the sun. Germans. They nod at her, but she looks away.

The store is another five blocks into town, but first she has to pass the side road to Gloria's where the steep bank of stairs leads to the hotel. Gloria and her husband could be sitting on their patio, and from there they would be able to spot her. If there is anyone Joan wants to avoid, it is Gloria.

The last time she saw her, they'd met on the street. Gloria reached out and touched Joan's arm. Her Spanish was quick and Joan couldn't understand her. She motioned toward the hotel and for Joan to wait. Gloria kept glancing back as she climbed the stairs. "Uno momento," she called, before disappearing inside. Joan stood on the curb and thought about leaving. She was just about to go, when she saw Gloria coming down the stairs with a book in her hands. She held it out to her as if it were sacred, dark eyes moist as she bit her lower lip. She spoke slowly to Joan with concern in her voice. "Under the bed?" Joan repeated, not sure that she was hearing right.

Gloria tried to give her a seventh-grade math book. There were worksheets sticking out from under its cover of fractions and colliding geometric shapes. Joan looked blankly into Gloria's face as she shook her head slowly. "El libro, no es mio." Gloria's expression turned to one of dismay. "Si, Señora," Gloria said, and offered her the book again. They looked at each other through a thick silence, as Joan continued to shake her head, no. She turned and left without the book. She left without even saying good-bye. "Señora," Gloria called, but Joan kept going. She walked clear through town in the wrong direction before she realized where she was.

The hotel patio is empty. Joan can see that someone is living in her old room. She crosses the street and out of view. The square that surrounds the well comes next. It is lined with benches and its nightly host of people. She walks past it with her eyes cast down, her hands tightened into fists. She moves with purpose; she does not drift. A man's voice calls out from behind her. It's Gloria's husband beckoning from the sidewalk.

Joan hurries up the block and ducks into the market where she pulls food from the single wall of shelves. She buys crackers and peanut butter, white bread and cornflakes, two packages of chocolate cupcakes, and six bottles of purified water. A white-haired man sits by the door with a newspaper. The woman at the counter looks at him urgently, as if she is trying to speak with her eyes. Joan stashes the food inside her pack and goes straight to the fruit stand across the street.

The weight of the packs pulls unevenly at her neck. She hikes them up as she heads for the square, but she isn't about to stop and fix it. She maneuvers her way through a group of tourists who are reading a menu that hangs in a window. The Beatles' "Yellow Submarine" blares from inside. The song lodges in her head, and she hums it like a mantra. Nobody calls her name from the square as she passes, though it seems like all the conversations stop.

She makes it as far as the construction site where she ducks inside the building to catch her breath. Dropping her packs, she sinks down to the floor. Iron rods stick up from the cement walls and frame the square of sky above her head. She eats a banana and two pieces of bread to try to quell her churning stomach as the moonlight creeps down the western wall. She tells herself that she has to keep going, that things will be fine once she's back on the beach. She shoulders her packs, focuses her mind on the nest and the fragile turtle eggs she will soon return to.

The light is so bright it could be day, as if the sun, not the moon, were in the sky. It casts a shadow on the road at her feet; a distorted self that mimes all her movements. A dog barks from somewhere in the hills, and she tries to stave off what she knows will come next; the scene in her head that plagues her each time she climbs the road out of town. Each time it is slightly different. Each time it leaves her feeling sick. Think about the turtles. Concentrate. Their size. Their shape. Their tiny ridged shells. Her legs move automatically along the curves of the road, but her thoughts slip out of pace with her feet. She can't keep it from happening again.

IT WAS NINE IN THE MORNING and already hot. The hills around her smelled like baked sage. She'd risen early to get a good start, having heard about a little-known beach that was far from town, but that had good snorkeling. She'd already gone what seemed a long way. The light-haired dog was with her on the road. It ran out ahead and crisscrossed the pavement. It sniffed at everything, nosing in the ditches and exploring the hills. Joan was content to lag behind. His curiosity made her feel grounded, lazy, and content. She heard a car on the road and called to the dog to slow down and wait for her. The car roared by, lifting a cloud of dust that settled on the tops of her white tennis shoes. She sang as she walked, her usual song. Her mother had sung it and now so did she. "Oh, what a beautiful morning, Oh, what a beautiful day . . ." She didn't even like the song but it came to her lips without any thought. "The corn is as high as an elephant's eye . . ." She rounded a bend and caught sun in her eyes. She raised her hand to block the glare; the dog, turning, waved back at her.

There were three Mexican boys standing on the road. The dog circled them with shy curiosity.

"Buenos dias," she said, as she approached.

"Buenos dias," replied the tallest of the three, making himself taller as he spoke.

He was lean and cocky with mischievous eyes. She thought he looked about twelve. The other two were younger; they looked away and giggled. The tall boy held a dead lizard by the tail. He laid it in the gravel for the dog to inspect. Its eyes were closed. It had snaky skin that sagged and wrinkled around its joints. The dog poked curiously at the carcass. Joan kept her distance and pretended to be impressed, which set off a round of banter and chiding. They pulled their slingshots from their pockets to reenact the kill. Each one claimed to have slung the fatal rock. Joan laughed with them and tried out her Spanish. She asked them questions about their families. They wanted to know how much their tennis shoes cost. She asked for directions to Mina Beach. The tall boy pointed up the road a bit and motioned a turn into what looked like a dump.

"La playa?" Joan asked in her overpronounced Spanish, with a look of disbelief on her face.

"Si, si," the boy laughed, and picked up the lizard.

Joan couldn't tell if he was joking or not, but thanked him anyway.

"Señorita," the tall boy called after her. "Buy us those shoes," he pointed, "with the lights when you walk." Joan turned, surprised by his boldness and his English. "He needs shoes," he said, shoving one of the younger boys toward her. "Just like those. Just like Micheal Jordan." And at that, they broke into peals of laughter.

JOAN IS HOT even though it is night. The shirt under her windbreaker sticks to her back, and her stomach rolls sickeningly. She wants to stop and rest, but can't. An urgency she can feel but not name forces her to keep moving. In the bright moonlight, everything appears infused with energy. The contrast of shadow and light is too sharp. She can see the contour of every hill, see the bark of the trees and their gangly shadows that inch their way along in the dirt. Her own shadow has grown close to her height; it walks even with her, stays firmly at her side.

Joan holds her breath in the dump, but she doesn't run through it. In the woods she walks fast. She tries humming "Oh, What a Beautiful Morning," but all she can see is the dog's panting tongue. A drip of water falls from it to the sand.

She can't move fast with the packs on the beach so she cuts down to the slope at the water's edge where the sand is hard from the weight of the waves. A curl of water hits the shore with a thud. It opens into a fan and rushes up the slope. Joan stands rigid in its midst. It swirls, pulling at her ankles as it drains back out to sea. She leaps to where the sand is dry, where she drops the packs and starts running down the beach.

The lines of her hut are clear in the moonlight, and the shape of her stick with the flipper is distinct. Also clear are the shapes in the sand, two small dark circles crawling to the sea. She kneels beside them. She picks one up. Its flippers keep moving like a wind-up toy. It looks different than she imagined yet familiar to her, as if a part of her always knew. She sets it down and watches it go. It struggles over the waves of sand. Anger and guilt wash over her, like the fans of water sliding over the sand. It had started without her. She should never have left.

At the nest, the fronds make a whispering sound as they jostle each other, set in motion by the turtles. A small stream of hatchlings is making its way out. Joan clears off the nest to ease their path. The sand at her feet churns and shifts as turtle backs and flippers emerge from the pit. She watches as they crawl away and wonders how they know which way to go. Can they see the water, or are they drawn to the sound of it? Maybe, somehow, they feel the sea through the sand, feel the movement of water currents through their flippers. But even if they can sense the sea, Joan wants to know how they know they belong there. She thinks that the knowledge may be carried like a gene, imprinted in each cell of the animal's body. What will happen when they reach the water if they have no mother's wake to follow, no one to teach them how to swim or find food? Joan wills the mother turtle to be offshore. She starts to cry, silent tears with no feeling, just water that her body can't hold anymore.

The moon is round and straight overhead. It is ringed with a halo that fills the sky. Some of the turtles seem confused, they head sideways down the beach. Joan herds the strays and puts them back on course, but there are so many that she has trouble keeping track of them.

She picks one up and reaches for another when a ghost crab zooms in and snatches it in its pincers. The crab drags it down a hole. Joan jumps backward as if she's been shocked, electricity pulsing up and down her arms. She looks over the sand. It is spotted with crabs. She runs screaming for the nest.

She pulls off her windbreaker and piles turtles on top of it. They crawl over each other, some flip onto their backs. Gathering up the bundle, she sprints for the sea. She dumps them out on the slope of sand where they roll and tumble, then are lifted by a wave. She wants to watch them, she wants to see where they go, but she dashes back to fill her jacket again.

The crabs are encroaching, taking turtles all around her. She runs for the nest. Everything is moving too fast.

Her thigh muscles burn. She feels clumsy and frantic and stuck in slow motion. She picks up the palm fronds discarded in the sand and goes into battle against the crabs. With a frond in each hand she slashes at the ground. From a distance she looks like a giant bird dancing alone under the moon. The crabs advance. They seem to be everywhere, closing in from every side. She swats and dips, then turns and falls, feels a new shell crack beneath her hand. She jerks it away and looks down at the turtle. Its shell is split, its neck is crooked, one of its flippers spasming. Joan hugs her stomach and vomits.

She senses its presence before her eyes take it in. The light-haired dog is watching her from the roof of the hut. The crabs surround her forming a circle. They dance in a ring, their pincers locked together. The dog jumps down with its paws outstretched, lands on all fours, and starts to bark. It circles the crabs and sniffs at them cautiously. It seems to be looking for a place to get through. "Here, boy," she whispers through her tears. He steps into the circle, his body shivering. His light hair is wet and sticking up in clumps around the snorkeling mask that's pushed up on his forehead. His eyes are framed by wet triangles of lashes, and his lips look blue from swimming too long. He has a towel wrapped around his narrow shoulders. He holds it closed with one hand in front of his chest. His other arm dangles down at his side. He is holding one blue snorkeling flipper. A drip of water falls from it to the sand.

WHEN JOAN WAKES UP the sun is high. It has nearly cleared the cliffs behind her and shines on the aqua green water of the cove. She sits up slowly. Sand falls from her hair and pours down her shirt. For a moment she's not sure where she is. Every pore of her body feels ripped wide open. She digs her toes into the wet sand and watches the humps grow and crack around the edges. They look like peanut butter cookies, the ones she used to bake all the time.

They had come to Mina Beach on a blistering day.

They'd met Mexican boys on the road who had been hunting, so he wanted a slingshot of his own, and why not mail them the shoes when they get home?

At the beach, he'd gone straight for the water carrying all of his snorkeling gear.

She stayed back in the shade in a small group of palm trees; she'd gotten too much sun on the hike from town.

She ate pineapple off the blade of his knife, her fingers sticky from the sweet tangy juice.

He came back and showed her a three-legged starfish.

He was hungry, and she made him a peanut butter sandwich. She told him that he should drink more water.

He convinced her to move to the other end of the cove because he wanted to try the snorkeling there. He pointed to an old palapa in the distance, said she could watch him from inside.

They picked up their things and walked down the beach.

He chattered excitedly about what he had seen. A school of narrow fish with long thin noses that hovered just below the surface of the water, and a dark brown fish with blue polka dots that looked like it would glow in the dark.

She spread the beach blanket inside the hut.

She rubbed more sunscreen on his back, then decided to make him wear his T-shirt in the water.

She left the door open so she could keep an eye on him. She could see him in the water close to shore, see the bright orange band around his air tube.

She lay on her side and propped her head in her hand. She opened her book, but she didn't read.

She thought about hammocks, how beautiful they looked, intricately woven with strong colorful threads.

A gentle breeze blew over her skin.

She let her head rest in the crook of her arm.

There was sand in her mouth.

The pages of her book flapped in the wind.

The sky was gray and the water was choppy.

She couldn't see him anywhere.

Garden Primitives

She jumped to her feet and ran down the shore where a blue snorkeling flipper rolled in the surf.

JOAN LIFTS HER CHIN from her chest. A low sound comes wrenching out of her mouth like the voice of her bowels or her liver or her spleen. The sun sparkles on the water. She wants to die where she sits, but her lungs keep breathing and her heart still beats. Her legs will take her back, but they'll move by sheer instinct.

→ *Mother Superior*

THE LONG SHIP BELLOWS as it leaves the harbor, bearing into the icy black lake, its taconite load at capacity. Nora, edging her thumbnail in pearl, stops to listen. She knocks her knuckle for luck against the board that's propping open her kitchen window. Wherever it's headed she hopes it gets there all in one. *The Emperor. The Henry Steinbrenner. The Edmund Fitzgerald.* In her fifty-six years at least a dozen have been lost, and who knows when the lake might claim another one, swallow it whole just like nothing.

She finishes her thumb and moves on to her index, slow strokes, taking her time. She's not going to show till after eight, though Don will be there at 7:30 flat. He'd been coming in every Sunday night. Why she'd never thought to go for his type, thinking steady meant boring instead of just steady. A lot of pain and trouble it would have saved her. Maybe one marriage instead of three, but who knows? People do what they do until they do something else. She'd always gone for the alley-cat type. The territorial, but roaming toms. Not that she didn't roam some herself. Fight fire with fire. She'd learned that young.

Again the ship's horn rolls through her kitchen, its sound going right through her, more solemn than the bells of St. Lucia's. There are times when, looking over the water, she thinks of the longboats and wooden schooners lying in complete darkness, hundreds and hundreds of feet below, the water too cold for the wood to even rot. The thin hem of the curtain flutters. The lake air smells like thawing ground and dog shit. Nora covers the rest of her nail in pearl, her hand spread on the green formica table under the light of a small lamp. Still good, she thinks, looking at her long fingers. Plenty of men have called them elegant. She holds her nails to her lips and blows.

Her neighbor's Doberman starts barking no end. Nora leans her head out the window, careful not to touch her nails. The dog is leashed to a spike in the dirt yard below, tugging to get to the chain-link fence that some kids are kicking a ball against. "Get out of here!" she belts, but they ignore her. With the palm of her hand, she unbolts the door and steps out on the wooden fire escape.

"Up yours," one says, and she moves toward the stairs. Twenty-nine years behind a bar, and nobody tangles with Nora long. The kids take off running between the houses, then disappear behind the boarded-up school. Why not turn it into a youth center? Give the damn kids somewhere to go. In her day, they spent their time downtown. There used to be a movie theater, no, two, and a place that sold sweets and popcorn next door. She remembers the department store with the balcony inside where you could look out over the whole floor. Trouble meant stealing the fake eggs out of refrigerators in the appliance department. And how they used to follow sailors down the sidewalk, trying to guess what country they came from. As busy a port as anywhere, with no ocean for over a thousand miles. But everything changed when the mines shut down, disabling the railroad, shipping, and all. Everything fell like a pyramid of glasses, the cloth yanked from underneath, but in slow motion so it was hard to keep track of the broken glass accumulating in the street. Sometimes it startled her to notice a sagging porch on a house that was nice once. Sometimes during a stretch of lake fog, it seemed there was nothing left of the city of Superior but six-foot rusty anchors and the gray ghost of its history.

A thin brown cigarette burning in the ashtray, and a glass of vodka just to get her mood up. Nora creases the paper to the crossword and jumble, folding the obituaries out of sight. Never pays to tempt bad news, though she gets hers like lightning to metal most often, even on a bluebird day: the phone call about her first husband's accident at the refinery, two others dead of heart attacks, the fire that razed her bar a few years back. But the first's death led the way to the second, the second eventually cleared room for the third, and the fire, well, that was a different sort of adjustment. At least her insurance had been up to date. There's always a good side if you can get to it.

Nora breezes through the word puzzles, checking the clock every so often. She wants to be just the right amount of late, enough to get Don looking toward the door. If there's one thing she knows, it's men. And men never want what's easy to get. She figures that deep down Don's no different, though on the surface he's a another breed. Owned and ran his own hardware store all those years. Kept it going even after the mall. It was a shame his kid not wanting to take it over. Stayed married to his wife and took care of her through her sickness. She recalls him coming into her bar back then. He'd order beer and sit by himself, never drinking past his fill. And though she could always tell when a guy was troubled, he never seemed interested in talking. At the time she thought he was acting too good, for her, her bar, her whole part of town. Now that she's getting to know him, she can see it's just that he's got a private side.

Well there then, Nora says to herself in the mirror, putting aside her eyeliner and blush. She fluffs up her copper red hair, arranging it to cover where her roots are showing. She'd decided on a navy skirt and a light blue sweater, not a plunger, but one that shows a little of what she's got. She runs coral orange over her lips, presses them together, and calls herself ready. Her house is tidy and her flowered coverlet smooth. If she reads it on him, she'll ask him up.

Not that it's really a date, Nora tells herself, stepping into the chilly night air. But hadn't she noticed how he kept showing up, and how his eyes would liven when she'd take the stool next to his? She could drive, of course, but this way it's left open for him to offer her a ride home again. She tightens the belt of her beige overcoat, making her street-shadow hourglass. The hedge is growing out its buds, the weather channel proving right again that spring's not going to be as late as last year. She turns up the avenue with its vacant lots and neon beer signs. It looks grubby tonight though it's no different than last. She's seeing it with Don's eyes, she thinks, coming over from Billings Park with its neat houses and lawns.

She wishes she'd had another bump to keep off the cold. The lake wind, after crossing miles of open water, is blowing on the back of her neck. Colder by the lake as always. The harbor still has a few ice floes, and there are large slabs piled against the footing of the bridge. Even ten miles out of town the weather has a different pattern. Sometimes she wonders why she's stayed on. When she was young, she had been set on moving someplace warm where there's palm trees and no snow.

The sidewalk beneath her feet rumbles. Some engineer driving like crazy. Someday she's going to go to Paris, take pictures of cathedrals, and have an artist draw her face. A vacation visit, to see it for herself. But mostly cities aren't her cup. Too much traffic, and all the people. In St. Paul, she couldn't tell direction for her life. It's the lake in her blood that gives her her bearings. It's frigid and it's lethal, but it's hers as much as anything. She can feel its pull even now, about a mile from her back.

There are only two prostitutes standing by the hotel tonight. Poor things. It's always struck her as the saddest fate. She can see the vacant lot ahead where her bar, The Superior, used to be. She clips open her change purse and fishes for a coin. She can never quite believe how tiny it looks, just a bare spot on the corner with no upward dimension, no walls to hold the memories together. Now it's just a nothing corner to angle through, a place to leave an empty beer bottle. She pitches a nickel onto the cracked cement slab.

The Anchor is her usual preference. She used to go there on nights off. It's the only one on the entire avenue that feels anything like right anymore. The Saunter Inn is a strip bar again, the Cave, a disco; she'd always hated The Dock, and Millie's got overrun by college kids. But the Anchor has kept itself up. It's still cluttered with glass floats, lanterns, and winches hanging from the ceiling, and all over the walls. There's the last photo taken of the *Benjamin Noble* before she became an un- solved mystery, and of course Josephine, the weathered figurehead behind the bar. All of it collected for who knows how long, all one big jumble like somebody's attic. She fluffs her hair and wipes the corners of her mouth with her pinky. "Don," she'll smile, looking sur- prised to see him.

"What's up, Nora? You surprised to see me?" Franklin asks from behind the bar, where he's flipping cards for solitaire. The bar's nearly empty, and no Don. Just Rose on her usual stool, a table eating burgers, and a few guys playing pool.

"You never surprise me," Nora says, adjusting her face into a smile. "It's like death in here."

Franklin reaches for the bottle of Smirnoff.

"Just a beer," she says, taking the stool at the end next to Rose. There's a small metal plate screwed into the bar that says "Sergio's Stool" in curly engraving. And it was his stool for as long as she can remember. Sergio and Rose were as regular as Josephine. Since he died, it's Rose all alone.

"How's things?" Nora asks, taking off her coat. "Did you play the organ at St. Michael's this morning?" Rose just nods and exhales smoke. Pool balls clack in the back room. Nora hears one drop and roll down the chute. Franklin sets her a coaster and a beer. "To Sergio," she says, lifting her glass, and Rose turns and smiles at her. She's been known to slap people off the stool who don't pay proper respect. "Pretty quiet," Nora says, sipping off the head. "Anyone been in?"

"Jack Mull, but he left with a bad stomach." Rose's words slur into each other.

"Could be flu, it's going around," Franklin says, emptying the ashtray before heading back to his cards.

"Could be that burger you cooked him." Rose's laugh is high and girlish. Half-cocked as she is, she forgets to put her hand up, and Nora can see her missing teeth.

Flu. Nora thinks of Don, hoping he's not out flat on his back. The bar door opens, and she turns her head, but it's only Carrie and Len. She used to hire Len to play at her bar. Providing a venue for the local talent was a part of the bar that she misses now. Rose and Sergio were a famous duo. They had a real name in their heyday, even opened for acts down in Chicago.

"How's tricks?" Len asks, leaning against the other end of the bar.

"I'm not talking to you till you move out of town," Nora says and turns a haughty cheek. She's told him a million times to move to the Cities, that he's wasting his talent staying in town.

Len blows her a kiss. "Aw, but you'd miss me." He takes his pitcher and glasses off of the bar, hefts the pitcher toward Rose. "To old Serg," he says.

Rose is staring into the kitchen where the red plastic burger baskets are stacked on a shelf. "Did you get supper?" Nora asks, feeling sorry for her, living glued to the stool like she does.

"It's got the value of a pork chop," Rose mumbles, swirling what's left of the ice in her glass.

That's Guinness, Nora thinks, but she isn't going to argue. She knows the way a drink warms and fills, takes away your appetite. She always eats something herself, though. She'd had herring and toast before doing her nails.

She knocks a cigarette from her pack, lights it, and slides the lighter back in its pouch. Men hate being sick alone, she thinks. No one to bring them a cold cloth or tea, fuss around like a private nurse. She pushes her glass forward for a refill. She's not really going to get drinking, in case Don still shows up. Cold air blows down the bar, but it's Phil, who's probably the last person she wants to see.

"Well, look at you all dolled up. What did you just come from—church?" He laughs and swings his bowleg over a stool, leaving a couple empty ones between them.

"Yeah, I did. I gave the sermon. Used you as an example of how to get to hell guaranteed."

Mother Superior

Rose hoots and slaps the bar. Nora rolls her cigarette coolly in the ashtray.

"Don't you two give me any trouble," Franklin says, setting a whiskey-seven in front of Phil.

"Who, me and Mother Superior?"

Nora raises an eyebrow and smirks. It annoys her when he calls her that. At least he's left off the ever-changing rest of it. Mother Superior and the Short Orders. Mother Superior and the Order-a-Beers. It started, of course, when she owned her bar, but it's not like The Superior even exists anymore. And it just seems wrong to use religious people in jokes.

She and Phil go back further than she cares to remember. Whole other lifetimes, some of it. In high school he'd been crackerjack smart. Could have gone on to anything. That's what kills her. Back then, she'd been ready to go on with him, but he'd turned down his scholarship for a job with the railroad.

"Plug the box, will you Franklin?" There's nothing like music to fill empty space, and she's feeling some both inside and out.

"Serious, what are you up to?" Phil asks.

"What makes you think I'm up to anything?"

Phil smiles into his drink.

"You always think you know something, don't you."

"Yep," he says, winking at her.

"Well, I'll tell you something you don't know then.

And that's when to mind your own business. Franklin, hon, pour me just a small bump."

Franklin pours her a solid Smirnoff. "Save me the trouble of getting up again," he says.

Bobby Darin is singing "Mack the Knife," from the jukebox. Nora taps her nails on the bar. She's always liked the swing of that song and how it rises to such a big ending.

"You ought to be nice to me. I've been sick as a dog," Phil says without taking the cigarette from his mouth.

"Bottle flu?"

"My ass," he says. "Serious, it's enough to make you pray for the end. What do you keep looking at the door for?"

Nora doesn't answer him. She wishes Rose wasn't in the bag. There's no talking to her after a certain point. She can see Carrie and Len in the mirror behind the bar, but they're sitting with their heads close.

"Ohhhh, I see," Phil keeps on.

"If you could see, you'd see I'm ignoring you."

"I see it. I'm just ignoring that you're ignoring me."

"For crying out loud. Don't you have any manners?"

Phil pats his pockets. "Guess I left 'em at home. Hey, Franklin, you got any manners for Nora?" He swivels his stool and looks around the bar. "Not much chance of finding any with this crowd. Where's Hamilton? Tired of slumming it?"

Mother Superior

Nora stubs out her cigarette. "Not another word. I won't listen to your bad-mouthing."

Phil runs his eyes up and down Nora, then bursts out laughing. "Oh God, Nora. You've got to be kidding. Don Hamilton? Isn't he a little honest for you?"

"If you don't shut it right now, I'll put this glass through your teeth."

"Enough," Franklin says, slapping his cards down.

Nora turns toward Rose whose chin is nodding, then motions to Franklin to top her drink. She can hear Phil snickering into his glass, and this isn't how she'd seen the night going at all. It's 9:30, and he's not going to show. Poor thing. She hopes he's not too bad off. She runs her finger down the side of her glass, clearing away stripes of fog, then lights another cigarette for thinking time.

"Franklin, hand me the phone book, would you?" She flips to the Hs and slides her finger down the column. There's his address, looking right at her. She belts up her coat and walks over to Phil.

"Give me your keys," she says holding out her hand.

"What for?"

"'Cause I'm asking." She nudges her hand closer.

"You're something," he says and drops them into her hand. "The things I do for you," he calls after her, but the door has already closed.

Nora adjusts the seat back and the mirror, then turns the key in Phil's old blue Chevy. Damn thing still has a broken muffler, and the car smells like dirty socks. The avenue is quiet. Beer signs blink. A plastic bag scuttles across the street. Something has let out at Grace Lutheran and people are turning to frown at her car. At times it seems like all that's left are the people who go to church and the people who go to bars. Of course there's a big crossover, too. She slows as she passes Louis' all-night diner, known for its gyros and walnut pancakes, but there's hardly a car, and no white Altima. Nora cracks the window to blow the stink out. She can't see how Phil can drive with the racket.

Her nerve is slipping so she takes the highway in the direction of the abandoned ore dock. Eighty feet tall and easily ten times as long, all a rusty latticework of beams. It's been out of service for so many years that she considers it her private place. It's where she goes when she needs to sort things through, a place to stare out at the never-ending water. She can see it ahead, looming into the lake. It's like a cathedral underneath, high arches marked with cryptic graffiti, and the constantly changing who-loves-who. But she makes up her mind before getting there. Why not? It would be a nice thing to do. Maybe she should pull in to the Stop-and-Shop to pick up a can of soup and some ginger ale. If it's his stomach, though, there'd be no point. She'll just check in and see if there's anything he needs. Let him know that he's not alone.

Mother Superior

The car rattles over the viaduct bridge. Beneath her the train tracks run twenty across. There are lines of un-hitched boxcars sitting idle, moonlight shining on their roofs. In Billings Park, the car sounds even louder. She could see herself living in a place like this, with room for a real garden, maybe some nice patio furniture.

She doesn't want Don to see her driving Phil's wreck so she leaves it parked around the corner. She can't be-lieve how quiet it gets as soon as she turns off the engine. Sunday-night quiet like people are already in bed, or sitting in their kitchens looking at next week's calendar. Don's yard is bordered with a flattop hedge, which makes her smile 'cause he wears his hair the same way. There's a light in the upstairs window, but the rest of the house is dark. Her footsteps sound funny going up his walk, and she wonders if maybe this wasn't such a good idea after all. What if he's sleeping and she wakes him up? But her feet keep moving toward the door, and her long pearled nail lands square on the doorbell.

Nora clears her throat and puts a hand to her hair. A light switches on, and she sees bare feet on the stairs, then the rest of Don in a thick navy bathrobe. The out-door light comes on, and there's Don's surprised face, peering at her from the other side of the window. He opens the door with his eyebrows still raised.

"Evening," she says, feeling suddenly shy. "I heard . . . Well, I thought that you might be needing something."

"Really," he says, his expression confused. He looks past her to the street, and then ushers her inside. He hangs her coat in the closet and draws the living room drapes before gesturing for her to sit. Nora takes a seat on an overstuffed sofa. "Can I get you a drink?" he offers, twisting his ring in a way that looks to her like nervousness.

"Vodka would be good. On ice if you have it."

Of course he has ice. What a stupid thing to say. Nora checks her face in her compact. There's a pretty clock ticking on the mantel, flanked by pictures of Don's family. She hears him crack an ice tray in the kitchen. There's a clean glass coffee table with magazines, and the newspaper's folded back to the half-filled-in crossword. Everything's as orderly as she'd expected. Don sets their drinks on coasters, hers mallards, his wood ducks.

"So," he says, sitting next to her. "I must say I'm a little surprised to see you." He looks down into his drink as he talks.

Nora wants a cigarette, but there are no ashtrays out, and the house smells never-smoked-in. It's quiet except for the ticking clock, and with Don sitting there she feels like she should explain.

"I got to thinking when you didn't show up tonight. I mean, I know how it is when you're not feeling right and you're all alone." She takes a swallow of her drink and sets it on the mallards. "How are you?" she asks.

"Fine. Maybe better since you showed up."

"You always say real nice things. I like that about you." Nora looks at her hands, then smooths her skirt. "Lily-of-the-Valley,"she says. "That's thirty-one across. All the long ones are spring flowers today."

"Really?" He touches her hand and smiles, then withdraws it and looks down at his feet. She's so happy now that she came to see him. He leans over and gives her a kiss on the cheek. "It's good you came by. You know it's been a long time."

"I just saw you last week," she smiles widely. He rests his hand lightly on her knee. Nora can feel her cheeks flush. He leans over and gives her a quick kiss on the mouth. Clearing his throat, he picks up his glass, but then puts it down without drinking. He takes her by the shoulders and kisses her long. First kisses can tell you a lot about a guy, and she likes how gentle he's being, no pushing tongue right off.

"I can't believe I'm doing this," he whispers into her neck.

"Ummm," she says, concentrating on the feel of his hand as it moves tentatively to her waist.

"I couldn't be the only one who wasn't able to resist," he says, all warm breath in her ear. After a long and rolling kiss, he starts leaning his weight into her. Nora closes her eyes and lets her body sink into the cushions. "I always wondered what I'd do if you offered, but I guess I'm no stronger than the rest of them."

"Ummm," Nora says, and then her eyes open. "Offered? Rest of who?"

"You know," he winks and leans back in.

She pulls away.

"Don't worry," he grins. "I'm okay with it, really."

Nora has seen that kind of grin before. She watches \big(133
her hand swipe his face.

"I don't know what kind of filth you've heard, or what you've made up in your own sick head."

"Wait. I'm sorry."

But she's off the couch.

"I didn't mean anything. I guess I just thought."

"No. Obviously you didn't think. I swear to God, Don Hamilton, don't you come around me ever."

Nora pulls away from the curb, not giving a damn about the loudness now, liking it in fact. She even wishes it were louder. She'd circle his block a thousand times. But she doesn't circle, she gets clean out of there.

The red lights are flashing and the arm lowers before she makes it up to the crossing, and now she'll have to sit and wait. The train approaches, taking its time. The boxcars squeak and rock in front of her. If she doubles back she could take the bridge, but she doesn't care enough to do it. Instead she pushes in the lighter, opens the window, and leans her head on the steering wheel. The air feels cold inside her ear where his wet tongue had been. She listens to the train creak and roll, heading out of town to who knows where. Anywhere sounds good. Des Moines. Kansas City.

The bar is warm, thick with fry-grease and smoke, and it's filled up since she left. She walks in straight-backed and calm, takes the only open stool which is next to Phil.

"Mother Superior returns," he says. "Roll out the red carpet."

"Pour me a long one," she says, loosening her belt, not even acknowledging. The vodka tastes like she's been waiting for it all her life. She closes her eyes and lets its heat fill her throat.

"You planning to give me back my keys?"

"Thanks," she says, sliding them over. She can feel Phil studying the side of her face, but she keeps her eyes forward or down in her drink. She knows that it won't take long. With every swallow she pushes Don deeper, drowning him, forcing him into darkness. Like the lake, she's not one to give up her dead. She keeps them lying in icy darkness, too deep, too cold, to rise to the surface.

Phil's watching her again, but he's not talking, and she's not about to invite him to. She lights a cigarette off the butt of her last, and sets to the work of drowning him further. A blue robe fluttering to the depths, sinking deeper and darker, till he's out of sight. Nora scans the room in the bar mirror, and realizes for the first time that the crowd is mostly kids.

"What's going on?" She nods her head toward the tables.

Franklin points to a sign over the register. It reads, "Philosopher's Night—2 fer 1 Pitchers—Every Sunday From 10:00 To Close."

"I know, I know," he says apologetically. "I need the business; I had to."

Nora tilts her head back, lets the ice hit her lip. She's no stranger to doing what you have to do. Even so, the Anchor courting college kids with cheap pitchers seems like more than she can stand right now. She looks down the bar. Rose is gone. There are kids on Rose and Sergio's stools playing dice. She orders another and it slides down like water.

"Take me home." Nora turns to Phil.

"You all right?"

"Yeah, I just got to get out of here."

"I'll finish this," he says, lifting a near-full glass.

"Take me home now."

Phil tosses a pile of clothes over the seat so Nora has a place to put her feet. "Meant to do laundry," he says, pulling into the street, the car roaring like they're going a hundred.

"They stink," she says, cracking the window.

"What do you expect? They're dirty." Nora rolls her eyes. "What, does your laundry smell like roses?" She doesn't answer him, she just watches the avenue swim by. She's thinking of telling him to drive her out to the ore dock, but no, she would want to be there alone. They idle at the light in front of the drugstore. Nora stares at the window display that hasn't changed in years: the foot bath, the toiletries, the stuffed rabbit on a chair. It looks shabby and yellowed like an old postcard. "What's up? You seem madder than a barrel full of monkeys." Phil snorts at his joke. Nora doesn't give. He shrugs, and they drive the rest of the way in silence.

"Come up," she says from the curb, before slamming the door shut. On her stoop, she hears the engine go silent. The Doberman's inside, barking like mad. Phil catches up to her at the top of the stairs as she's digging in her bag for keys. He puts his hands tentatively on her hips and leans his head into the back of her neck.

"To what do I owe this private audience?" he whispers.

Nora rests her forehead against the door. "Shut up, Phil. Just shut up."

❧ *This Third Year of Returning*

I WOULD STAY HERE where the calm is vast, but I know that tonight I must go. The veil is stretched thin, a fragile membrane. It parts as easily as a tongue through wetness, and then the first skin of remembering and the jarring recollection of crushing pain. Steering wheel against chest bones, forehead to glass. The shock of how easily steel can crumple. A last catch of bubbling breath, and I am borne up, or through, or beyond.

There are others.

Like a black cloud we roll across the sky, our heat lightning rising, blurring stars. From darkness the boundaries of shape emerge. Far below, the wide river snakes. And from creases of land, the streams flow toward it, joining it like leaf vein to rib.

There is no feeling of air passing. Speed exists as memory, and the whole splits into named segments—darkness, river. Nor is there sound. No whistle of wind, or night bird. Stone silence is everywhere.

The fields have been harvested. They stretch from the river, a gray-black quilt pulled over spent shoulders of earth. Then the first small river towns, their sprinkle of lights clustered on the banks.

We thin. Our numbers veer off in black streaks like falling stars that hold no light. And the recollection of what it is to wish.

She is not far now.

There, the lock and dam that segment the river, dropping the water to a low plane. The limestone bluff where I hunted fossils as a boy, their chalky spirals flash in my memory. I cut away early, not yet ready to enter, this time, this third year of returning.

Black against black falling toward a wooded hill. The approaching treetops, an arterial maze, as everything constricts and divides further, splitting me into so many fragments.

I linger in an oak tree's high branches. A gnarled burl. Bark. Leaf. Squirrel. It natters from a lower limb, tail twitching, but it has no voice. Soon will come the torrent, the visual flood of color and texture crowded with random memory. This is what it is to go back.

Skimming the tops of bare trees that sink into ravines and then rise again to meet me. An owl swivels its head as I pass. I am the shadow in its eye. Then a car's taillights along the dark highway. I remember this road in the dead of summer. Heat rising in sheets from the pavement. I remember how a shirt will stick to vinyl.

Lower, I thread between rough-barked tree trunks over the forest floor of leaf and needle bed. On a grassy rise, a small fire burns. I recall the sound that sends sparks skyward. Closer, and there are quick flashes of light. A camera held in a woman's hand. She is a maiden in a moss-green gown. He, a knight, posing with a sword. It is the eve of the dead and disguised. The woman shrugs a chill off her neck. She lowers her camera and looks into the darkness. The fire flares, and I am gone.

Down a slope and across an open field, where brittle husks dangle from cut stalks. A deer gnawing a withered cob lifts its neck and stiffens. Its ears prick alert. I recall the rustling sound of October as the wind tosses the dry husks. In a farmhouse window, a single light burns. I pass the pane of yellow glass, and an old man looks up from his book.

She used to paint whiskers on her face, or wear plastic skeletons dangling from her ears. I would sit at the table shuffling though work papers or scrolling the computer screen. I would watch her rise eagerly at the sound of the doorbell. Now and then she would call for me to come see the tiger or the mop-head rag doll. Sometimes I would.

On my first return, the porch light was off. That year, there were no jack-o-lanterns along the porch rail.

This Third Year of Returning

And the children avoided her unwelcoming sidewalk, passing it for the next orange-lit house. When I entered, I found shades pulled on a darkened room. She lay on the couch with the cat on her chest. The cat lifted its head and stared. She was bag-eyed and thin. She shifted and pushed the cat to the floor, her brow wrinkled in fitful half-sleep. Set prominently on the mantel was a newly framed photo, taken at our wedding just a few years before. Her figurine dress. My charcoal suit.

I shatter completely under the first streetlight, overwhelmed by delineations of line and color. The fluted edge of a yellow oak leaf. The granules in the sidewalk sparkle where it lies. In the street, the sharp rocks pressed into the tar are a million slivers of light and shadow. And a fallen peppermint lying in the grass, its red and white swirls, dizzying.

Flanking the boulevards are small groups of children. A young ghost waddles tentatively, carrying a pillowcase. Two boys with drawn-on stubble streak across the lawn, while a red cape flaps in the silent night. I remember wet breath behind a plastic mask, the smell of a jack-o-lantern's burning lid. And the leaves lining curbs, feather-lobed and elliptic, my feet swishing through them, kicking up the dust smell, always leaving stems stuck in my laces.

There are others here. Many others. One shadows a crying child dressed like a green bean. One moves with malintent, swooping down from a rooftop. I pass behind houses, chain-link fences, yards. An empty swing sways. A dog bares its teeth. One winter night she couldn't stop crying and I never knew why, though I held her for hours.

I pass the brick high school where we first met, its windows looming flat and empty. One of the doors is splattered with egg. And in the parking lot there are no cars, just dim halos of light on the blacktop. It was there that I came to know her. The feel of her breast. What things made her scoff.

We were married here in this rose garden, surrounded by perfumed balls of color: scarlet, tangerine, canary, pearl. The garden lies in darkness now, the bushes dormant under flat-topped rose cones that cast shadows on the ground. The fountain is boxed under plywood for the winter. On the hill at the other end of the gardens, a circle of teenagers pass a bottle. Their cigarettes glow orange and then dim in the night. And I am close now to where I need to go.

On her block, strings of children crisscross the street in a pantomime rush toward the next lit house. I pass a young father who waits on the sidewalk. He tenses his shoulders and turns up his collar.

Her porch light is off.

I rise up to the shingled valley between dormer and roof. The porch, dark again, as on my second return.

This Third Year of Returning

When I entered the house then, it was shadowed and empty, everything the same. I left, scanning the neighborhoods, hoping to find her car, but I could not. So I waited, here in this very spot, watching the limbs of the yellowed elm rise and sway in a soundless dance. It was late when her car lights swung into the drive. She walked slowly across the lawn below me, costumed as the three of clubs. Instead of going into the house, she sat down in the wicker porch chair. She, a bent card, a club creased at her waist. She sat in the dark staring at the empty street where gusts of wind blew brittle leaves in circles. I, next to her, watched her cry, and smoke, and begin to cry all over again, her face turning red, her shoulders shaking, and I could do nothing but leave her there as the thin edge of dawn appeared.

I enter her house for the third time and find the living room dark and still. The couch. The portrait on the mantel. There are no magazines scattered, no stray dishes. I remember how it used to be, ashtrays and mail on the coffee table, life's details collected on the surfaces of things. But then, set on the floor by the entrance, I discover the wooden salad bowl. Inside are small candy bars and a bramble of sucker sticks.

In the kitchen, the alley light throws a square across the floor. There are dishes left in the midst of washing. They lie below the water's filmy surface, one thin patch of bubbles floating.

Garden Primitives

Passing the stairway, I notice a dim bar of light beneath her door.

She is there. A scarf over the bedside lamp sheds a mottled gold and yellow light. She lies on her back, the white sheet to her hips, his hand tracing the curve of her belly. I recognize the flush on her cheeks, and the warm hunger in her eyes.

The cat stares at the wall where I linger. Touch her softly, just barely, with your fingertips. Yes. Between her breasts like that. Pay attention to her breathing; she won't tell you what she wants. I watch her nipple rise hard and pink, and I remember the feel of it against my tongue. The man smiles. She speaks to him.

She rolls on her hip and touches his face. I know the wet shine in her eyes. His lips move in a rush of words near her ear. Her hand covers his mouth. She laughs.

And I am the dim flicker in her bedside window. This night, taking my last leave.

This Third Year of Returning

→ *You're So Simple*

THERE COMES A TIME on northern lakes when the
evening glows with a pale light, but when the color of
the trees has drained away, leaving them black silhou-
ettes against the sky. Dane watches the lake from the
dock behind the boathouse where he goes to smoke
and get away from his father. He sees the black forest
and its reflection in the water, how together they form
a seamless mountain of darkness, jagged and double-
edged. A whistle signals the approach of a train that will
pass the lake near the small resort, four cabins tucked
under tall pines. It sounds over the trees and across the
water where it falls, dissolving like a soft mist. A fish
jumps. A screen door bangs. Dane flicks his cigarette
into the lake.

"Mom," Cheryl's daughter Amy chides, "you're not
supposed to let the door bang."

"No sass," Cheryl says, her arms full. Could she help

it that the door had slammed shut? It wasn't as bad as the kids trampling in and out all day. Bang. Bang. Whiffs of fish and sunshine, leaving sand and small puddles on the floor while they dirty dishes or use the bathroom, before running back to the small beach and the swimming area roped off by Clorox-bottle buoys.

She carries a grocery bag in each arm; sodas, marshmallows, chocolate bars, graham crackers, napkins—enough for everyone, she hopes. It's their traditional last-night bonfire. The honeymooners in cabin four she is certain won't come, but Emmet and Mave Holmberg, the older couple in three, had said they would. And then there's the Johnsons. It still doesn't seem right to call them that, since the Johnsons used to mean Bob and Laura, and now it means Bob and Roberta.

For years, she and Larry had been coming to Whispering Pines, often in the same part of August as the Johnsons, whose boys nearly matched their girls in age. They hadn't seen them for two summers, so when the blue station wagon with Illinois plates pulled up to cabin two, she'd left the breakfast dishes half-done in the sink. Wiping her wet hands on her shorts, she'd crossed the lawn as the car doors opened, tennis-shoed feet and arms emerging. Laura with long, thick, black hair and half the size she used to be. Not Laura. A nanny for the kids? But just as she was about to ask the obvious question, Bob gave her a flattening look.

"Roberta, Cheryl. Cheryl, Roberta."

She'd eyed their matching gold wedding bands.

LARRY IN BED, adjusting his pillow and finding his place in the mystery he was reading. "Things change," was all he'd said.

"I can't believe Bob's not with Laura. And for a younger woman. God. What is she? Thirty-five, maybe?"

"That's only ten years difference," he'd shrugged, "and who knows what happened anyway?"

"Why are you defending him?"

"I'm not defending anybody. What's the deal?"

"I'm not blind. You tell me."

"Cheryl," he'd said.

"Right." She'd rolled her back to him, aware of the fat around her waist, her thick thighs, and her short, practical hair.

CHERYL HIKES UP her grocery bags. If Roberta had given birth to two kids, she'd look a little different too. And Bob, he'd adored Laura, the way he'd take her hand, or touch her cheek. He'd even serenade her on his guitar.

Emmet Holmberg, leaning on his deck rail, sees Cheryl trudging over the lawn that joins the cabins to the lake. The train whistle has faded away, but it's left a faint echo in his mind. He breathes in the piney air and looks out at the darkening water. He has never liked dusk, he doesn't like endings, and though Mave has tried to make him change his perspective and see the sunset as the beginning of night and not as the end of day, it has never worked. Endings make him angry.

He watches Cheryl dump her load on the picnic table. She reminds him of a big fly, the way she's always buzzing around everyone, her own kids and the Johnson boys, too. At least she's not right next door. Then again, that would be better than listening to Bob Johnson fight with his boy, Dane. Just the sound of the boy's defiant voice brings up memories of his Benny. The fights and then the silence after them. Which is worse is hard to say. He fingers the pocket where he keeps his inhaler. Yesterday's fight had brought on a terrible attack. He had pumped his inhaler into his mouth as the shouting got louder and meaner. Finally, he'd headed for the boat. Reverse. Out of the wooden slip. Pointing her nose down the lake. Throttle wide open. Got to get out of earshot.

Cheryl folds the paper bags and wedges them between the picnic table planks. Shit.

"Larry," she hollers, "I forgot matches."

She sees Emmet standing on his deck, moths fluttering around the light behind his head. Strange man, so standoffish. Every day, out in his boat, putting along the shore with a fishing pole, his shoulders stooped, his blue canvas hat. But Amy likes him, running down to the fish house every time he comes in with a stringer. "Mom, when he cut open its stomach there was a baby fish skeleton inside." And she seems to like Mave, too, who's pleasant enough, but hardly company, always reading or knitting on her deck.

"Emmet," Cheryl waves, "bring your flashlight. There isn't any moon tonight."

Larry parks a wheelbarrow full of firewood near the beach.

"Where are the girls?" Cheryl asks.

"Coming. Angela's reading in her room. She left the pans soaking, said she'd finish them later."

His wife's eyes flick up to the sky.

"Give her some space, Cheryl, she's twelve years old."

"I know exactly how old she is." She has seen the way Angela moons around Dane and she'd just as soon have her stay a child a bit longer. "She promised she was going to come."

"I know, I was there." Larry piles the firewood in a crisscross stack. "More?"

"And matches, okay?"

Larry can hear Bob and his son yelling as he bumps the empty wheelbarrow over the grass toward the wood-shed between their cabins. And there she is, framed in a rectangle of light. Roberta, rubbing lotion on her face. Roberta, stretching her calves on a tree before jogging.

You're So Simple

Roberta, shucking corn on her deck. Roberta, with her shirt unbuttoned, beckoning to him from behind the boathouse. He wishes. Cheryl, tight-lipped, has been snubbing her all week. She could eat Roberta alive. No wonder he feels protective. She's sweet, maybe a little shy, but that could be more about Bob than anything. Guys like Bob take up a lot of room.

The birch logs clunk into the wheelbarrow. He looks toward her window casually, but she either hasn't heard him, or doesn't care. She pulls a sweatshirt over her head. While her face is covered he stares at her breasts. Not large, but not small either. Everything about her is tight and compact. He wouldn't mind eating her alive. The window goes dark. He stoops for a log.

His own kitchen window splays light across the grass and into the low boughs of a jack pine. He pushes the wheelbarrow into the light. Angela's back is bent over the sink. Her colt-like legs. Her elbow scrubbing. She's changing so fast these days. She straightens, and he pushes out of the light, feeling kind of like a jerk. First Roberta, and now his own daughter, both unaware of him watching.

Angela gives the roast pan a final rinse and turns it upside down in the dish rack. She goes back to the open window that she'd fled when she heard the rumble of the wheelbarrow, but the Johnsons' cabin is quiet now. She couldn't tell what the fight was about. Dane's dad was a creep, no doubt about it. "Don't let him get under your skin," she'd told Dane, feeling wise as the words came out, even though they belonged to her mother.

Dane. She loves the sound of his name. In her notebook, she has written it over and over, surrounding their initials with a heart. If only, she wishes, he'd give her a sign that he liked her, too. She watches the Johnsons file out their front door; Roberta and Jeff are loaded down, flashlight beams cutting all over the place. Then, Dane's dad carrying lawn chairs and a guitar. But no Dane. Their screen door bangs shut. Angela slides the roast pan back into the dishwater in case anyone tries to fetch her down to the fire.

Larry parks the wheelbarrow. The matches. He has forgotten the matches. Cheryl is crouched, laying logs in the sand.

"Shoot," he says, patting his pockets. "I must have dropped the matches out there." Why is he lying? He'd better get a grip. Good thing they'll be going home in the morning. Out of sight, out of mind, he hopes.

Bob bends over, lighter in hand. "I've got it. Let me."

Cheryl smiles up at him.

Like he's the cavalry, Larry thinks. Always the ladies' man. Come on. A high school math teacher whose big thrill is coaching football?

Roberta is setting up a small bar on the picnic table, a liter of gin, tonic, an ice chest, and half-moons of lime fanned on a plate. Larry watches her run her hand through her hair. She turns, and he looks toward the fire pit.

"Need a drink?" she asks.

"Who, what?"

She smiles and tilts her head toward him. As if there were more to the question, maybe.

"Not quite yet." Though he really could use one. And what was that look all about? He wonders if she knows he had been outside her window, or if it was obvious she was starring in his fantasies.

"I'll take one, sugar," Bob says, slipping his arm confidently around her waist and putting his mouth on the back of her neck. That neck, Larry thinks. He spreads a blanket in the sand next to Cheryl, who is on all fours blowing at the fire. He reaches out and pats her rump.

"Dad spanked Mom, Dad spanked Mom," Amy singsongs and laughs.

Cheryl looks at him over her shoulder and lifts a wary eyebrow.

"Angela."

"Shit, you scared me."

"Scaredy cat," Dane says.

Angela presses her forehead to the window screen and cups her hands around her eyes.

"Let's go," he says.

"I have to go to the bonfire."

"What for? . . . Come on, I thought you wanted to."

"Where are you?"

"Invisible."

"My mom will kill me if I don't go." He says nothing. She still can't see him. "You were fighting with your dad again."

"Grounded. I told old Bob I wasn't going to sit around some stupid fire and sing camp songs."

"Oh, good one."

"I'm not two years old."

"Well, duh. Neither am I."

"Here I am in bumfuck nowhere and old Bob grounds me. Like where am I going to go . . . except the train bridge."

"I can't. I want to. Just wait until later."

"Come on, Angela . . . Annnngeelaaaa."

"Okay, I'll just go down for a while and then I'll tell them I don't feel good."

"I'm going without you."

"No. Wait. I promise, really."

THE SCREEN DOOR SLAPS SHUT behind Angela. She can taste the wood smoke of the bonfire that glows orange and gold in the darkness. Amy is twirling in circles on the beach. She knows she is chanting "star

You're So Simple

light, star bright," because she taught her to do it while spinning. Part of Angela wants to spin along with her, but Amy doesn't even wish, she's too young. Dane's little brother is poking at the leeches that he tortures with salt in a coffee can. The grown-ups are circled around the fire. The Holmbergs on lawn chairs, her parents' backs, and Dane's dad and Roberta all glowing yellow. Mrs. Johnson? Roberta? She doesn't know what she's supposed to call her. She's so pretty, and she's got perfect nails. Dane's lucky, she thinks, though there's no way she'd say so. He hates Roberta nearly as much as he hates his dad.

"She's a wimp," he'd told her the other night when they'd snuck out to the boathouse after everyone was asleep. "She's always in her room with the door shut. Probably playing with herself." Then he'd lowered his voice imitating his father, "Roberta needs a place of her own with all of us men in the house." He didn't care. He had a room in the basement now which was a lot more convenient. "If you know what I mean." She hadn't known what he'd meant.

"Do you miss your mom?" she'd finally asked after chickening out a bunch of times.

"Yeah, right," he'd scoffed, flicking his cigarette, the glowing cherry arcing over the water, fizzling into the black lake.

Dane.

"Come sit," Cheryl says, patting the blanket next to her. But Angela edges in next to her dad.

"Another round?" Bob offers, rocking easily up to his feet and stretching his arms in athletic circles. "Angela? Soda?"

He doesn't look anything like Dane, Angela thinks, watching watching him pass fresh drinks around to everyone, even Mr. Holmberg. Her mom has already had a couple; she can tell by how loud her voice is and the way she's moving all exaggerated. Mrs. Holmberg is the only one not drinking. Her hands are busy with her knitting needles. They click and flash in the firelight.

"Socks for the St."Socks for the St. Joseph's home for children." And no, she doesn't really need better light. "It's a feeling thing more than a seeing thing."

"Last year it was scarves," Mr. Holmberg says. "She's going to have those kids so bound in wool that they won't be able to walk."

"I think it's wonderful," Roberta says. "Those kids must need a lot of attention."

"Most kids do," Cheryl smiles.

Angela wants to turn around so she can keep an eye on the Johnsons' cabin. How long is she going to have to sit there? Smoke is getting in her hair and she'd just washed it with her new cream rinse.

"They do need special care," Mave says to Roberta, tugging at her line of yarn. Poor girl. The other one,

You're So Simple

Cheryl, had been harping about her all week. Yesterday, marching right up on the deck—couldn't she see she was trying to read?—all red in the face and uninvited, standing there with her hands on her hips. "That boy needs his mother," she'd said under her breath. And gone on about some Laura girl until it finally dawned on her that Roberta wasn't their mother. And didn't she agree that what Bob had done was terrible? "She's just too young and inexperienced . . . She's not equipped to handle those boys." All of this coming on the tail of a huge screaming match at the Johnsons'. It had gotten Emmet so upset that he'd had a horrible wheezing fit. "I should tell that fellow a thing or two," he'd said. "I've got half a mind to go on over there." Instead, he'd gone out on the water and stayed away so long that she'd had to hold supper.

Amy and Jeff are screaming and laughing, chasing each other with dead leeches.

"Mom," Angela says, feeling protective of the honeymooners, "they shouldn't go near those people's cabin."

Her mom yells, "Come on kids," but doesn't get any response.

A dim light is glowing through the window shade of the honeymooners' cabin. Angela watches for movement, but as usual there is none. She hasn't even seen them once. Their red car, all muddy around the bottom, hasn't moved from the gravel pad. "They're probably fucking their brains out," Dane said. "Oh, right," she'd countered, "you're so simple." She can't really picture what they are doing, but whatever it is she thinks it's romantic and that they should be left alone.

Bob is tuning his guitar. "S'mores!" he shouts. The kids come running. He fiddles with his strings absent-mindedly while watching Jeff set to work, choosing his roasting stick and his spot in the fire. Just like Laura. He can practically see her, the way she'd turn hers carefully until it was perfectly brown all over. Then, pop. The whole thing would be in her mouth. Just watching her eat used to make him hungry, used to make his own food taste better. Christ. Why does she keep coming to mind? He'd been stupid to bring Roberta and the boys here.

"Not so close to the fire," Cheryl warns Jeff, and then gives Larry an I-told-you-so look.

Jeff was fine, but Bob saw the look that Cheryl gave Larry.

"Sit back," he says, but Jeff doesn't. "Damn it, I said sit back." He grabs the boy's collar and yanks him from the fire.

Emmet Holmberg's leg begins to bounce. Mave stops her knitting to place her hand on his thigh.

"Angela," her mother says, offering her marshmallows and a stick. "Aren't you going to have any, baby?"

She's drunk for sure, calling her that. Angela yawns and shakes her head. "I don't feel very good. I'm going

You're So Simple

to go read." But Dane's dad is playing her favorite, "Blowin' in the Wind." The words, she thinks, seem sad and important. She kind of wants to stay, but what if Dane leaves without her?

"You can read in the car tomorrow," her mother coaxes.

She turns to her dad with pleading eyes.

"Don't stay up late," he says, patting her leg. She bends to kiss him, tucking her hair behind her ears.

Suddenly his little girl again. He watches her walk away from the fire, her figure blending into the darkness until he can't make her out anymore. Across from him, Roberta is staring at the fire, her chin resting on her knees. He takes a big gulp of his gin and watches the firelight feather her forehead.

Roberta's cheeks are hot from the fire and gin. There's a small cavern between two logs. It's white-orange pure heat and she can't take her eyes from it. She'll stay there in her little cavern. She has nothing to say to these people. "There probably won't be anyone we used to know," Bob had said. "It will be good for the boys to go back." He's the one, she thinks, who needed to come, to prove that his life was normal again. It's another one of his little tests, and she understands, in a way. Not next year, though. She will not come back here.

"Oh, it was sad . . . So sad! . . . It was sad . . . Too bad! . . . It was sad when the great ship went down . . ." Bob is

Garden Primitives

teaching Amy the words to "The Titanic." She's all smiles and big eyes. "Husbands and wives, little children lost their lives . . ."

"That's horrible, Bob," Cheryl accuses.

Jeff leans into Roberta's leg, and she puts her arm around his shoulder. At least he will be with her like that. Dane, well, it's best to leave him alone. Whatever he has to work out is between him and Bob.

"What about counseling," she'd brought up again that morning.

"Don't start," Bob had said.

"But things seem worse between you two. Dane's mad or shut down all the time. I'm worried. It's not normal."

"Tell me, what's normal?"

"You know what I mean."

The fire shifts, changing the shape of her cavern. She's only vaguely aware of the singing. Maybe she really should call Laura about Dane. She has her phone number in her wallet. Bob would never forgive her. It must have been awful for Dane to discover his mother's affair. Traumatic, walking in on them like that. No, she couldn't possibly call Laura.

"What?"

"I said, darling, have you got a request?"

Roberta shakes her head, no.

"All right, this one's for you," Bob says. And he serenades her with "You Are So Beautiful." Amy giggles.

You're So Simple

"Dad," Jeff whines, obviously embarrassed, chocolate streaked around his mouth.

Cheryl throws balled-up Hershey wrappers into the fire. She watches them burn blue and crinkle into ash. Singing to Roberta? Unbelievable. Can't he see he's making a fool of himself?

ANGELA BRUSHES HER HAIR in the mirror and applies her watermelon-flavored lip gloss. It's their last night together and she's hoping Dane will kiss her, though he hasn't tried anything. She latches her bedroom door from inside, turns off the light, and climbs out the window, leaving the screen in place but not hooked.

"Dane," she whispers, but there aren't any lights on and she thinks maybe he's left without her.

"Dane?" He lunges for the screen.

"Shit, you creep."

"Told you you were chicken. Look at this," he says, holding a bottle against the screen. "They took the gin, but they left the vodka."

"What if they notice?"

"What if?"

She can hear them singing from the road. It's cold, and to Angela their families around the fire look suddenly warm and comforting. The road is dark, the flanking woods darker. Dane lopes fearlessly along. When they round the bend Angela turns on her flashlight even though she's worried he'll think she's a baby. He doesn't taunt her. He doesn't say anything. He just takes another long swig of vodka.

"Aren't you worried they're going to find out?" she asks. Dane lights a cigarette. "Are you drunk?"

"Are you drunk?" he mimics. "Try some, it's goooood."

Angela puts the bottle to her lips. It smells horrible, but she takes a sip.

"See," he says.

"I've had better," she manages, as it burns disgusting down her throat.

IT'S COLD at the picnic table away from the fire, and quiet, Larry thinks, since the kids were sent to bed. He squeezes limes into plastic cups. He really doesn't need another drink, but then again, none of them do. Roberta has got her head on Bob's shoulder. Mave knits. Cheryl is smoking one of Bob's cigarettes, a sure sign that she's all in. A log pops orange sparks into the darkness. The booze has got Emmet talking anyway. Larry hands the drinks around.

"Roberta's a good shot with the birds," Bob says. "She got more grouse than I did last fall."

"You hunt?" Cheryl says to Roberta.

"My dad taught me. I've always liked it. Mostly it's being in the woods."

"But killing things? How could you?" Cheryl presses.

"I don't really see anything wrong with it, as long as you eat what you shoot," Larry says.

Cheryl rolls her eyes. "Come on, Larry. You've never hunted. You've always hated the idea."

"That's not my point."

"Your point is . . . ?"

Roberta lies down with her head in Bob's lap. He strokes her hair like he's petting a cat.

"Deer was my thing, but that was years ago," Emmet says.

"The big ones," Bob agrees. "It's head to head, you and the animal. You've got to be still and totally prepared." He aims an imaginary gun into the fire. "If you're lucky one will step right out in front of you. Boom."

Emmet nods. "I know what you mean. I just don't have the taste for it anymore."

"How could you kill a deer?" Cheryl sneers.

"Please. Spare me the Bambi crap," Bob says. He has just about had it with Cheryl's attitude.

"What people don't understand is that it needs to be done," Emmet says to Cheryl across the fire.

"Not to mention venison steaks," Bob laughs.

Cheryl watches him stroke Roberta's hair. He lifts his eyes and she meets them straight on.

"Don't you feel any guilt at all?" she blurts.

They stare at each other in silence.

Garden Primitives

Jeff appears in the firelight. Cheryl cups her cigarette behind her back.

"Dad, Dane's not in the cabin."

"Jesus Christ," Bob says through his teeth. All he'd wanted was a quiet family vacation, fun time for Roberta and the boys.

"It's okay, Jeff, go on back," Roberta says sitting up. When Jeff has gone, she turns to Bob. "He's probably just down at the boathouse again."

"Did I not say, stay in the cabin? It's pretty clear, stay-in-the-cabin."

Cheryl sighs audibly. "God knows, he has been through a lot. Maybe you need to have some patience."

Cheryl's face swims before Bob's eyes. "I should pitch his clothes right out the door. We'll see how far he gets on his own."

Emmet Holmberg's leg is bouncing again.

"You don't mean that," Roberta says in a calming voice.

"You don't mean that," he mimics her. "If I'd pulled half the shit that kid tries to pull, I wouldn't be here to tell you about it."

Hear, hear, Larry thinks.

"Divorce is hard on children," Cheryl says defiantly.

That's my girl, Larry smiles into his cup. She's gonna let him have it now.

"Oh yeah, it's hard. It's hard on everyone. Ask his damn mother how hard it is."

You're So Simple

"I won't listen to you say anything bad about Laura."
There. At last she'd said her name.

"Fine. Plug your ears. She's a goddamn whore."

Emmet reaches for his pocket.

"Bob," Larry cautions, "take it easy."

"Don't you, of all people, tell me how to act. I'd like to see you try to deal with Dane."

"And you're doing such a good job of it?" Cheryl says, feeling her blood racing now. "We're all sick and tired of listening to you fight. You both need counseling, is what you need."

"You goddamn women and your goddamn counseling." Bob glares at Cheryl and then at Roberta. "What Dane needs is a kick in the ass."

Emmet cups his hands over his mouth and starts pumping his inhaler.

"Beat him up. Way to go, Bob." Cheryl says. "If Laura could hear you she'd be appalled."

"He's alive, isn't he?" Emmet wheezes.

Mave's knitting needles go still.

"You don't have a clue, do you?" Emmet pauses, sucking in air. "Shot yourself deer, ever seen a dead boy?"

"Emmet, don't." Mave reaches for his arm, but he shrugs her away.

"They don't talk back, I'll give you that, but they don't do anything, understand? You going to pick out the suit to bury him in? Sure, you don't even know what size . . ." His voice chokes off and he bends over his inhaler.

A LOG FALLS. The Holmbergs' screen door bangs shut.

Bob stands at the picnic table, weaving slightly as he pours himself a drink. He turns to offer Roberta one, but she has taken her blanket and left.

A train whistle carries over the water once, and then sounds again.

"Jesus," Bob says, plunking down on the bench. "What the hell got into him? Did you hear me say anything about wanting the kid dead?"

"DID YOU HEAR THAT?" Angela says.

They are standing on the car bridge that spans the banks of the railroad bed. Angela leans over the concrete guardrail. Her flashlight shines a dull circle on the tracks. She can hear the distant whistle of the train.

"Dare me?" Dane says, climbing onto the barrier.

"I'm sure. Get down."

"Bok bok." He lifts his legs like a chicken, and flaps one arm while the other holds the vodka.

"It's coming from that way," Angela says, crossing over to the other guardrail. "Look," she points.

At the bend in the tracks, the sky brightens, then light hits the top of the trees and the outside rail begins

You're So Simple

to shine. She can feel the thrumming in her feet. The gleam of light is now on both rails, running toward her like thin rays of fire.

"Funky, funky chicken," Dane crows, hopping around on the guardrail behind her. He flaps his arm, throws his head back, and drinks. "Yahoo!"

Angela is mesmerized by the lines of light racing toward her on the metal rails. The trees and the sky are full of white light, and the train hammers around the bend. Blinding light. She has to half-shut her eyes. Wind roars past her ears and her hair flies up in a blast of hot air, as the train engines barrel under the bridge, light and metal on metal, screaming.

Then darkness.

She can barely make out the shapes of the boxcars. They slide beneath her, creaking and swaying, gigantic, pushing cold air from the railbed. She can't see the end of the train, just the cars directly below her, lumbering out of the blackness like a nightmare.

Angela shivers, and turns around. "Hey," she calls. "Where are you? Come on." She listens for the scrape of his shoe, searches the darkness for his glowing cigarette. Nothing anywhere. The creaking train.

She scans the length of the bridge with her flashlight, then crosses back to where she'd left him. The train squeaks and rumbles below.

"This isn't funny. I'm not kidding."

She shines her light on the backs of the boxcars, their weight rolling and shifting beneath her. She sweeps it along the scrubby banks, then over the gravel railroad bed.

BOB WALKS BACK to the fire shaking his head. He sits and pulls a blanket around his shoulders.

Larry pulls a marshmallow stick from the fire and holds its burning end in the air. The flame goes out. Smoke twists into the sky. "Well I've had about as much fun as I can take. Where's the water bucket? Did you bring it down?

Cheryl stares mutely at the flames.

"The bucket?" he repeats.

"The porch, I suppose. Is it my job to keep track of everything?"

Larry walks into the darkness.

Bob's face is turned toward the sky. "Stars make me crazy," he says. "Billions of them going on and on. Look at 'em. Christ. Makes you feel like an ant."

"You're not who you used to be," Cheryl says in a whisper. "You used to be . . . I don't know."

"Like what's the point anyway?" Bob mutters to the stars.

A faint shriek drifts over the water. Cheryl's head snaps to attention. "Did you hear that?"

Bob swallows a gulp of gin.

You're So Simple

"What was it? Listen. There it is again."

"Sounds like a loon," he says.

"Loons don't sound like that."

"Well, some kind of owl then. How should I know?"

→ *Still Life*

RAIN FELL IN THE NIGHT. It woke you up. You ate strawberries and watched lightning through the window. The storm beat in unpredictable rhythms, showing glimpses of your neighborhood like so many x-rays. The electric flashes pulled off the night's skin to bare the blue-boned skeletons of houses. You watched as if secrets might be revealed, but the flashes of light were too quick and all that was left was the rumble of thunder, and you wished for arms to lie down into, a warm chest, and the heartbeat of another mammal.

In the shower, hot water beats down on your shoulders. It pours over your face and into your mouth. You stand for a long, long time. No one expects you to be anywhere. It's been months since you were laid off from your job, since you last needed to set your alarm clock. Your weeks have lost their boxy shape of weekends edging a block of work. Steam rises in plumes and shrouds your mirror. You wipe it with a towel and look at your re-flection, study the face that others see. You turn your head to the side, still looking in the glass, your pupil wedged in the corner of your eye. You can feel the muscles pull. You wipe the mirror again and look head-on, try out expressions you think are yours. A slight smile and your head tilts. A wider one forms lines in the corners of your eyes. You try to probe into your own dark pupils, but they don't let you in, they only probe back. After a time, your face looks foreign, like a word that's been repeated over and over, until it loses its meaning and becomes pure sound. You have to look away. You turn off the light, fearing the oval of pale-skinned features, the mouth and the hair that is framed in the glass.

The coffee smells thick and you pop up the toast. The slices are brown. Their texture is like sand. You rub them with butter straight from the stick, carry a plate and a mug to the chair by the window. Crumbs are stuck to the soles of your feet, and you brush them away before settling into the cushion.

There is moist air coming through the screen. All that's left of the storm are small pools of water formed along the sidewalk cracks. They draw children off course from their daycare walk. They stop to inspect floating worms. They stomp in the water with rubber boots.

Your window looks out on a dingy house. It has warped shingles and mismatched siding. Over the winter, the view drove you crazy, a monotone study, a wash in gray: gray house, gray sky, exhaust-covered snowbanks, and filthy cars. Even the birds looked dirty to you.

The house looks abandoned but you know it isn't. Often you've been awakened in the middle of the night by shouts or red lights spinning on your walls. You can't see into the rooms of the house. Sheets are hung where there should be shades. There's a plywood square tacked over one window. You were a witness to that night of destruction. It was 2 A.M. when you broke from your dream. The sheet was gone from the picture window. A man and a woman kept furniture between them. He was stripped to the waist, white flesh in the lamplight. She, in a housecoat. They circled each other. She picked up a vase and sent it crashing through the window. You called the police, but by the time they came she had fled down the street and the house was dark. The patrol car slowed, swept the bushes with its searchlight, then kept on going. The wheels never stopped.

There are two boys who live on the upper floor. Some mornings you see them crawl in front of the sheet and stand on the windowsill looking out. One is half a head taller than the other. Their brown stomachs round over white underpants. You want to protect them, to cover their ears, to pull the glass shards out of their dreams. There's no movement at all in the house this morning. The sheets hang like blank canvases. Squirrels run across the roof.

Cars speed by below your window. The fullness of the air makes them sound like cloth ripping. The light on your answering machine is blinking. The call must have come while you were in the shower. You press PLAY thinking about job prospects. Instead you hear a child's voice. It's Emily, your friends' five-year-old daughter, whose paintings are taped to your refrigerator door. Her voice is excited. "Guess what?" she says, as if expecting to get a response. "I lost my tooth, the one that was wiggly. It came out when I was brushing my teeth. I have to put it under my pillow 'cause then Mom says the tooth fairy will come." Her mother's voice is muffled in the background. "Mom says, do you want to come by later?" Leslie takes the phone. "Hi toots, we'll be around. She is so excited about her tooth, she says she's got a window for her tongue to look out of. Anyway . . . I have to run. She needs to be to kindergarten by 1:00. Hope to see you." The machine beeps.

You remember what it was like to lose a tooth, how you would work it with your fingers until one side

Garden Primitives

would pull up. The edge that used to be planted in your gums jagged and sharp against the tip of your tongue. At school you'd sit at your metal desk and play with it without using your hands. When it was barely attached anymore you'd gather your bravery and yank it out, hold it in your palm like a precious little seed. You'd touch your tongue, triumphant, in the empty space, feel the squishy spot, taste a hint of blood.

Your own teeth are wide and straight. They're your second set. You won't grow a third. You run your tongue over the surfaces in your mouth and think about your teeth, how you take them for granted. They work to crunch crackers, sink into dense chocolate, break thread, and snip corn kernels clean from the cob. You chew and chew, giving them no thought until accidentally you chew yourself, your finger or tongue or your soft inner cheek, your eyes flinging open from the pain. You've been startled, even scared, by the strength of your jaw. It's like carrying a weapon concealed in your head, and it's been there for so long you forget and grow careless. You could, at your bidding, inflict serious wounds. You possess the strength to tear raw flesh from bone.

The sky has grown darker, congealed into forms. Ridges and scallops hang over the city. What's above you is clearly the bottom of something else. You want to be in

Still Life

it so you get dressed. You choose old clothes that hide your shape. They are unrestricting, your own soft armor.

People on the street move purposefully. You don't engage them. You pass invisibly like the wind that blows squalls across the puddles. You move as if rolling; you're a marble, a cat's-eye. Your path is dictated by traffic and whim. You cross with green lights, enter neighborhoods with old trees that rise over the street in cathedral arches.

You look at the houses where other people live. They are set off from you by green squares of grass. There's a garden hose stretched along a stone walkway and a mower abandoned in the middle of a yard. You can smell the wet grass and the patches of clover. A bed of red tulips lines a wooden front porch; in the gray light they glow as if lit from inside. There's a porch swing and chairs and a stack of tied newspapers. You sidestep a tricycle with water on the seat. You don't see people, just the objects from their lives. It's a life that's hard to picture for yourself. One of napping children, children sitting in grocery carts, the running of benign errands that add up to a home.

A mailman works toward you on the other side of the street. He holds letters sorted between his fingers. You can hear the lids of the metal boxes close, hear the snap of the mail slots as they spring shut. You imagine the envelopes scattered in an entry, and you wonder if someone will stoop for them, if they'll leaf through each one with anticipation and watch for their name in familiar pen.

You meander along sidewalks, around corners, down curbs, until you hit the open block of the park. You climb up a hill that overlooks downtown, the skyline that keeps on growing. The tall buildings burn yellow in the smudged charcoal sky. They cluster together, compete for prominence, reflect each other in their glass facades. They look like jeweled minglers at a cocktail party.

You remember a time when there was only one skyscraper. On a field trip in grade school you were warned not to throw anything from the top. A penny, the guide said, could kill someone below. As you stood with your fingers laced through the wire fence, you tried to imagine a tiny coin falling through the sky onto somebody's head. If you'd had one, you'd have been tempted to drop it, too young to understand such abstractions.

You walk through the grass down the back of the hill. Your path curves among new dandelion heads. The museum borders one side of the park. Its wide staircase

Still Life

appears to narrow as it rises to columns that tower around the entry.

The heavy doors fall shut behind you. The air has the density of a temple. You walk with your hands curled in your pockets. Your feet brush over the polished floor.

You travel through landscapes and admire how pigment and the turn of a bristle can evoke an atmosphere beyond what is seen. The water of the lake looks cold. You can nearly smell the fallen pine needles, sense picnickers on a blanket who share your view. You amble slowly between the frames, stop before a villa baking in noon light. You imagine the life behind its stone walls, a cavelike kitchen with abandoned lunch dishes, peeled potatoes on the counter in a pot of water. Roads and rivers curve into the paintings and you want to follow them, to see around the bends.

You cross into a hall lined with still lifes. You pause before paintings of red and green apples, a lemon half-peeled, a vase of peonies. You ponder the textures of familiar objects and the compositions within each frame, but your eyes are drawn to the free-form lines of the empty spaces between things.

You enter a gallery that's wide and square. Gilded frames catch patches of light and shadows nest in the carved-out hollows. The paintings are filled with bare-breasted women. They have long rippled hair. Their eyes roll toward the sky. Above them float cherubs with wings on their backs. They seem smug with judgment in their realm of clouds. Standing among the women, you feel your cheeks flush. You think what bothers you is their vulnerable posture, rooted to the ground, when the power is in the sky. But it's their skin that you keep staring at until you realize that it's too white, and their cheeks, their elbows, and their tiny perfect toes are painted in a soft pink tone. They are grown women wearing the skin of infants.

Downstairs you find a room of ancient Greek art. The pieces are carved from veined, white marble. On the walls, the title plates are all marked B.C. You can't really grasp the ages of the pieces, the centuries of caring that have kept them intact.

There is a statue of a woman in the corner of the gallery. Her body is draped in a marble gown that falls so naturally you believe she has knees. The statue is missing its arms and its head, and the toes of one of its feet are gone. You wonder where she's been throughout the years and how it was that she came to be broken. Perhaps she lost her head in the siege of a temple, pushed from her place by a conquering people. Or the accidents may have been benign, clumsy mistakes in the hands of admirers

Still Life

Maybe weather and time, or natural faults in the stone have made her look as she does today. There's a flat oval where her neck once was. It sparkles like quartz, and you want to touch it, but there's a guard in the room and he's watching you. You linger in the gallery until he leaves. From across the room she looks like an oak, her gown a covering of heavy bark. You walk over and touch the cool stone. It's both smooth and coarse under your fingers.

On your way out you stop at the gift shop, taken with the small birds on display in the window. They are painted bright colors, glossy pinks, blues, and greens. They turn on their strings with the moving air current. You ask to see one. It covers your hand. It is practically weightless, though made out of clay. You buy two. They are wrapped for you in white tissue paper. You unwrap one as soon as you get outside. The colors expand against the gray sky.

The clock on your dresser reads 5:30. You mark down the job rejection that came in the mail in the notebook on your desk where you keep track of such things. You put on a record of pipe music from the Andes. It blows through your rooms, and you fill a pot with water, put it on the stove to boil for pasta. You'll cook yourself a meal with lots of garlic, maybe even have a salad on the side. While you wait for the water, you sweep your floor and smooth the sheets on your unmade bed. You hang a colored bird in the window by your chair and watch it glide as the evening sky dims.

Your friends' door is open so you just walk in. Leslie greets you with a hug and Tom pours you red wine. The three of you sit at the wooden kitchen table where you set your glass over a familiar scar and let each other in on the passing of your day. Your faces ring around the light of a candle. Your backs and the rest of the room are in darkness. There's a bowl between you filled with fruit and shadows that bounce with the flame when Leslie laughs from her belly. Emily has already been put to bed. They show you her tooth that they swapped for two quarters. It looks barely used in your open hand.

You enter her room by the glow of her night-light. The floor is a mess of clothes and toys. You pick your way to the side of her bed. Her body is curled in a small sleeping mound. Her hair's in yellow tangles across her pillow.

From out on the walk a passerby might notice, framed through panes of amber light, a woman bending over a dreaming child.

Still Life

You take a painted bird out of your satchel and leave it on her nightstand with a note signed *love*.

→ *The Only Course*

LIFE JACKETS. Spare hose. Sidewalk salt. Rope. And boxes in the rafters not opened for years. Gloria rummaged through the clutter of her garage for something small and powerful. On the rake were hanging last year's leaves, curled and brown like sleeping bats. Manley's electric hedge trimmers. The truck she wouldn't use. Sitting in the driver's seat felt as foreign as waking on his side of the bed. The storm windows leaned in stacks. The antique gas can they'd bought in Michigan. The cool dankness of the garage was a childhood game of hide-and-seek. *Inside, crouching by a greasy canvas tarp. Outside, sharp sunlight on pebbles and grass.* "Memory is often triggered by smell." She'd heard that on the radio. She settled on a blue nylon stuff-sack. It had the musty odor particular to the hold of a boat. *Manley's feet in tennis shoes on the cockpit seat, steering with the tiller in the crook of his knee.*

In the kitchen, she tested the sack again. *The swing of the boom. The flutter of sheets. Taut. Riding the wind again. The wind blowing in her hair.* She set the sack with her purse on the counter so she wouldn't forget to bring it to the home, then gathered her dust rags and furniture polish.

Her dusting routine began with Houdini, the first antique that she and Manley kept, though they'd bought it to resell in the early days of their business. *Bought in Deerlake, Wisconsin. 1951?* She circled her dust rag around the clock's face. *An estate sale . . . or was it an auction?* She stopped dusting and closed her eyes to help remember. Nothing, until they were on the road. *The clock strapped down in the back of the truck, wrapped in blankets and tied down tight, her head craning back from the cab to make sure it wasn't going anywhere. Manley laughing. "Relax, Glo," he'd said. "What do you think we've got, Houdini back there?"*

The clock was the first piece that they'd named. It became a tradition as they drove through the countryside buying pieces to sell in their shop. For some they imagined fanciful histories as well. Greta Garbo's footstool. Ben Franklin's mother's butter churn. The ordinary things, the "quick sales," were all called Charlie or Jack. *Manley standing in the truck bed. "Hey, Glo, hand up that Charlie."*

Esmeralda, their couch, was a high-backed Queen Anne. Ralph Waldo a bookcase, Titi a lamp. Now, each piece demanded its own story. Gloria felt surrounded.

The rag in her hand rode Esmeralda's wooden curves. *An estate sale? Chrimini. He would know. Places. Names. Facts were easy for him.* She was more likely to recall weather or conversation, to retain a general sense of atmosphere. But Manley was getting harder to reach. His brain was like a deteriorating house where the doors to the rooms were often stuck shut, locking pieces of their life away.

The dust rag continued its habitual course. In the hall, a framed lithograph of a Great Lakes schooner, its bow slicing frothy waves. *I could bring him home for Thanksgiving. Manley winking across the table. The smell of his head on the pillow next to hers.* In the office, the desktop, the arms of a chair, one of Manley's best model ships. Gloria blew along its rigging, causing its open white sails to sway.

Quiet circled the office walls and filled Gloria's ears with ringing. *If I never let him out of my sight . . . Last winter, carrying groceries to the house. He, through the kitchen window flapping his arm. A bird with its wing on fire. Finally, his arm under water, her bag of groceries lying in the snow.* "Remember to turn off the stove," her sign had said . . . *Her eyes focused on the doctor's desk lamp. A silver pen in his breast pocket.* "Your husband needs professional care. You have to think about his best interests."

He would die first. That's how she'd always imagined it. It would be his heart, and come on like an earthquake. Then, after a moment of violent shaking, her life would be changed irrevocably. She thought she had

The Only Course

prepared herself for the worst. Not this. Not his slow drifting on a merciless tide, one day within reach, the next day gone again.

The rag hung down from Gloria's hand. Her fingers rubbed worried circles on the fabric, a habit from childhood, an unconscious action whenever she didn't know what to do. The ringing in her ears—*for heaven's sake*—the telephone on top of the desk. Gloria reached over and picked up the receiver.

"Lorraine . . . No, she had it right. I switched to tomorrow since that's our anniversary . . . Thanks . . . Forty-seven . . . I suppose it is. It doesn't seem that long to me."

OUT THE KITCHEN WINDOW it was a fine fall morning, a deep blue sky with high clouds that floated across Gloria's windowpane. Running hot water in the sink, she adds soap and slides in her breakfast dishes. *More tomatoes are ready to be picked.* Twisting a pink sponge inside her coffee cup, rinsing it, and turning it over in the dish rack. *The pile of dry leaves she had raked.* Her hand searching the bottom of the sink for silverware. *He bowling her over from behind. Leaves in her shirt. His face above hers. The sky hazy buttermilk beyond his shoulders.* A squirrel runs across a tree limb and leaps off the end onto the roof of the garage. Tiny soap bubbles popping on her wrists. A streak of movement ending in a scrabble of orange leaves. She could feel the weight of dread in her legs. *He's getting worse. The doctor had said it. Cortical functioning. Tangled neurofibers.* She couldn't keep the words straight. *How can a man forget half of his life? Half of my life? It is my life, too.*

MANLEY WAS DRESSED in a white shirt and trousers— he had always been a neat man—and he smiled at Gloria from his chair by the window. "Hello, dear," she said, and bent to kiss him, then pulled up her usual chair. "It's a beautiful day," she started cheerfully, "windy but the sun is warm."

"Ah, Glo," Manley said wistfully and turned his head toward the window. "How much longer for this war?"

"Honey. Darling. There is no war." *Korea, maybe, was that where his mind was?*

He didn't speak again. He seemed intent on something out the window. Gloria watched the side of his face; a muscle moved slightly in his cheek. His hand ran over the spindles of his chair, testing each for solidity. *His hand without knowing, feeling for workmanship.*

"I've brought you something," Gloria said, determined to keep a positive attitude. "I found this in the garage today." She held the stuff-sack to her nose and breathed in the musty odor. "It smells just like the *Dally-O-Day.*" Manley took the bag from her and set it in his lap. "Smell it," she urged, and he held it to his nose. "What do you say? It's the *Dally-O* isn't it?"

The Only Course

"I know," he said, and gave her his wink.

Gloria felt lifted by a wave of excitement. "Our first boat . . . Do you remember? . . . Light green hull . . . Small but fast, you always said."

"Dally-O-Day," Manley repeated, pausing between each word. His mouth spread into a soft wide grin. "A beauty . . . Strong double masts . . . Big twins."

"It was a sloop, Manley, our very first. We took her out to the Bear Islands after we got . . ."

"Two masts. Two masts." Manley wagged his finger. Gloria felt the wave she'd been riding flatten out under her. Manley kept shaking his finger. *What?* She turned to look over her shoulder. There sat a model ship, its two masts glued firmly in place.

"It's all right," she said, "it's all right," and took his hand between hers. She stroked his fingers until he calmed down. "The first time we went to the Bear Islands," she began, "on the *Dally-O-Day,* it was early June." She hesitated. She felt responsible for remembering it right. "It was summer," she began again. And she described her memories. The way she'd first been afraid when the boat heeled. The humpbacked islands rising up in the distance. "You burnt the pancakes."

Manley laughed.

Gloria leaned forward and lowered her voice. "We tried to make love in the dinghy." Manley nodded, but then turned away. His fingers scratched at his big loose ear.

"Storms?" he asked.

"No. It was beautiful."

"Storms," he said again, and then yawned and closed his eyes.

It's like reading a story to a child. He adds nothing, he contradicts nothing, as if I'm not talking about his own life.

THE NIGHT WAS SWIRLING wind and moonlight. Gloria pulled the living room shades. She took out Manley's anniversary gift, a cardigan she'd knitted from soft gray wool. All that was left was to sew on the buttons. She'd found them months ago in an antique shop. They were silver, embossed with clipper ships. Wetting a piece of thread. Pulling it through the eye of the needle. *Light rain falling as she pulled up the anchor line. Angry. They'd argued about whether to leave or stay. Gray sky. Seven hours to port. Manley insisting that they go, wanting to be back for some flea market. Rain pattering against her yellow slicker. Their course to the northwest. Westerly wind. Sails trimmed to a port beat. Silence between them all morning. "We'll be fine, Glo," he'd said. "We'll make good time with this wind." But she knew the danger of the lake in late season, how sudden storms bore down from the northeast, deadly storms, and he knew it, too. The rain falling harder. The swells rising. "Coming about hard alee," Manley ordered. Uncleating the jib sheet. Bow crossing the wind. Retrimming the sail to a starboard beat. Tacking should*

The Only Course

not have been necessary. She eyed the telltales flying stiffly from the shrouds. The wind had shifted around to the north. Behind her, she could no longer see land. The waves now whitecapped, causing the bow to rise high and slam into the troughs, throwing sheets of spray. The motion jarring her neck and head. With binoculars she could see mainland dead ahead. She focused all her will toward the thin dark strip. But off their beam the sky had turned purple. Both of them tied to lifelines now. The wind too strong to keep both sails up. The deck slick as ice as she uncleated the jib halyard, her pulse pounding in her ears. "We'll have to reef the main," Manley hollered, his voice flying away with the spray. Her eyes on the telltales. Wind gusting northeast. She hated him more than she ever thought possible. She focused all her energy on the dark strip of land. Just let us get there. Please let us get there. Wind screaming through the rigging. Manley tight-jawed, his hand on the tiller. Gale force gusts and she radioed mayday, just to let someone know they were out there. She'd never felt so alone, so aware of her life and the possibility that it could end then and there. The wave hitting them straight abeam. The boat broaching onto her side. Slow motion. The boat righting. She looked at Manley who stared blankly for a second. "Let out the main," he commanded as he pulled on the tiller to align the wind dead astern. "We're going to have to run with the wind." The main sheet speeding out through her fingers. Their course now heading away from land, out into miles of open water. Her head unwilling to turn from the mainland. "Are you crazy?" she shouted. "Where the hell are we going?"

"It's our only course," he shot back. "Gloria . . . Look at me. Trust me, Glo." The bow surfed the back of the waves crashing down into the troughs. "Watch the boom. I'll try to keep her from jibing." The bow as it nosedived into the water. Slow motion. This is it. The deck emerging. Water careening from its sides. "All we can do is ride it out." Her fingers made circles on the fabric of the couch.

DAWN'S ORANGE LIGHT filled Gloria's room, and she stretched her arms over her head. Languidly, she moved, mostly asleep though in her dreaming she was wide awake. She was a child, up to her knees in water. Searching the streambed, she tried not to move, tried not to ripple the water or make sand clouds with her feet. She was eight so convincingly that she'd have been shocked by her face in a mirror. Orange was everywhere. More awake now, she saw it. Soft and tranquil, orange enveloped her. Patches of orange on cream-colored walls. Orange in the air above her bed like great plates of stained glass that rotated lazily. Mandarin, marigold, orange vermillion. *Beautiful.* Orange trailed around her outstretched arms until she folded them back into sleep.

Gloria woke again at 7:15. The sky outside her window was a flat even blue. She lay on her back and looked at the ceiling. There were traces of the orange plates of glass in her mind, but she couldn't remember what she'd seen or felt, only that there had been something extra-ordinary. She rolled over to face Manley's pillow. "Happy Anniversary, dear," she whispered.

They were young, speeding across the South Dakota prairie, the wind whipping through the car's open windows. Holding hands, neither wanting to let go, so that when Manley went to shift gears, their hands together worked the stick. The Hershey bar she'd bought him as a wedding gift when they stopped at a gas station. The sun on his face as she watched him through the plate glass window. He, leaning casually against the car, talking to the kid who was pumping gas.

What else? Think. A warm fall afternoon. Kids on the schoolground across the street. The justice of the peace, tall and stringy. Yawning. He had tiny teeth. Manley, nervous, circling his shoulders as if his sports coat were too tight. What was the judge's name? Gary Thomas, Thomp-son, maybe not Gary.

FILTER. Coffee can. Four rounded scoops. Gloria listened to the tap water fill the glass pot. She had recently seen a TV show on overcoming disabilities. A blind woman had demonstrated how to pour liquid by listening to its rising pitch. Gloria closed her eyes and tried to discern when the pot was nearly full. Water ran out all over her hand.

Dark blue wrapping paper. A yellow ribbon. Gloria took a Hershey bar from her purse and tied it into the bow on the box. *"Glo, you shouldn't have."* *Manley slowly eating the chocolate, every year pretending to ignore the rest of the gift.*

She rang Manley's phone but he didn't answer. She tried the nurse's desk and was told that he was still asleep. "He had a rough night," the nurse said, assuring Gloria that he was fine now.

"Would you remind him that I have a hair appointment? I'll be there after his lunch."

"How's THE ANNIVERSARY GIRL?" Lorraine asked, her comb poised above Gloria's wet head.

"Good. And you?"

"Fall is my time of year. Good riddance to heat and send the kids back to school." The two exchanged smiles in the mirror.

"And Manley, how is he coming along?"

"He's all right. The same."

"Do you want anything special?"

His limbs were getting weaker. Degenerative. Irreversible. The words contained no hope. People are beating terminal illness by laughing.

Lorraine was watching her in the mirror.

"I'm sorry. Just a cut and curl. But leave me a little height on top. Manley likes it better that way."

Lorraine gave Gloria a sympathetic frown. She combed up sections of her hair and snipped them off with her

The Only Course

silver shears. Tufts of hair like small wet feathers fell to her cape and the pink linoleum floor. "I hope you're taking care of yourself," Lorraine said. "You know when Curt left me . . . Well, you remember. You've got to pick yourself up and go on."

Go on? Go where?

Lorraine led Gloria to the dryer and brought her a styrofoam cup filled with coffee. She gave her shoulder a little pinch. "Cheer up, love. You've got a lot to be thankful for."

The dryer blew hot air around Gloria's ears. *Manley smiling. Fingering his new sweater. Fawning over the silver buttons.* She settled into the comfort of the vinyl chair. Marilee Dobb's laugh pierced the room. Jeanne Highgate was getting her hair dyed and going on about how Ralph still thought it was natural. Gloria took in the beauty parlor's smell, its particular odor of flowery shampoo mixed with astringent curling solution. The mood around her was cheerful and humming, light and infectious like champagne bubbles, and she felt her spirit rise up on the effervescent energy of women's vanity.

Gloria met the cool wind and the sunshine with a vigor that she hadn't felt for weeks. As she drove, she watched familiar landmarks pass by. Parker Lane to Hicks to County Road 12 that ran parallel to the railroad tracks. Birch trees lined the road, their bright tops bent in the wind, brushing yellow across a cobalt sky.

The light was red at the grain elevator's intersection. Gloria stopped though there was no traffic. She was looking at the unhitched railroad cars when a flock of birds lit into the sky. They rose from the tracks as if all of one body, sunlight flashing against their wings. They turned, folding their wings in concert, blinked small against the sky, dipped low, spread their wings, their pattern growing large. *An incredible moving mosaic.* She wished there were someone with her who had seen it also. She would describe the birds to Manley. *They flew up flashing in the sun. Beautiful.*

Gloria pushed through the tinted glass doors into the heavy smell of pine-scented cleaner mingled with cafeteria food. It hung around her like a fog. *The same smell no matter which season.* It seemed part of the very paint on the walls, the lounge furniture, and the tile floor. Even the papers at the front desk she knew would have that smell on them. But she was determined to keep her good mood.

Manley was asleep in his chair, head back, lips parted. Gloria adjusted the blinds, letting slats of sunlight into the room. She pulled her chair up next to his and set the gift box in his lap. Manley stirred and snorted awake. "Happy Anniversary, dear," she said, feeling her heart full of love for him. She gathered his hand between her own. Manley looked at her curiously. Furrows slowly deepened in his brow and he tried to pull his hand away.

The Only Course

"It's okay, dear. Did I startle you?"

"Let go," he demanded, and jerked his hand free. He stood, dropping the gift to the floor.

"Manley, what's wrong?"

"Get back," he said, the chair now forming a barrier between them.

"It's me. Gloria." She extended her hand, but he only drew away from her.

His jaw tight. His eyes narrow. His hands grasping the back of the chair. The gift upside down on the floor between them.

"Nurse!" Gloria called as she fled the room.

The nurse came in with Gloria behind her. "Now Mr. Lillihan, what seems to be the matter? Come and lie down." She patted the bed. Manley edged toward the bed eyeing Gloria suspiciously.

"Here now, lie back. Is that better, dear? Look, your wife has brought you a present. How sweet, there's a candy bar tied in the bow." She retrieved the package from the floor, but Manley wouldn't take it from her.

"He doesn't know who I am," Gloria whispered, "does he?" She stared, unable to take her eyes from him. The nurse led her into the hall.

"He had a bad night last night," the nurse said. "I heard he did a bit of wandering. Why don't you come back tomorrow after he has had a good rest."

CLOUDS DRAGGED in front of the sun and cast long shadows across the garden, darkening everything, chilling Gloria's skin. She reached into the yellowing leaves and tugged a fat tomato free. Her head felt fuzzy with tiredness. *The nurse sitting with her in the hallway. The worn green carpet at her feet. "He has been up and down before,"* she'd said.

There was a pile of tomatoes in the grass. *Where in the world did I leave my basket?* She tried to load the tomatoes into her arms, but they kept spilling over onto the ground. "For heaven's sake," she blurted out angrily.

The sun broke free low in the west and flooded the yard with golden light. Everything appeared to glow, the leaves and the trees were bathed in succulence. *Damn tomatoes. Stupid tomatoes.*

SHE WASN'T ABLE TO EAT the chicken she cooked. She tried toast, but it burnt while she stood at the counter. She tried to watch television, tried to knit, but she kept losing count of her stitches. Tick . . . Tick. Houdini seemed loud. Tick . . . the yellow light of the lamp, cone-shaped on the wall . . . Tick . . . the magazines on the table lying as she'd left them days ago . . . Tick . . . She walked down the hall to the bedroom and closed the door against the sound. Lying curled on her side, sleep wouldn't come. Her fingers toyed with the hem of her pillowcase. The alarm clock read 9:17. In her robe, she wandered around her house, touching objects in the dark. A book. The waxy leaves of a plant. Crossing back from room to room. Circling without direction.

All was dead-still. Houdini ticked. A car's headlights slid across the window shade. In the kitchen the tiny blue pilot light burned. A rush of wind blew against the house, and Gloria sank down against the refrigerator. Slowly, the tears dropped from her eyes. She wept until there was nothing left but her ragged breathing and tear-soaked sleeves.

Tick . . . Gloria lifted her face from her arms. Her feet were alabaster in a swath of moonlight that angled through the back door window. Pulling herself up, she followed the light that lay across the kitchen floor. She opened the door to the dust smell of autumn, to swaying trees and clattering leaves. She hesitated with her hand on the screen door latch, then opened it, and the wind flung it wide.

BENEATH HER FEET, the grass was hard and cold. The night was wild with breath and moon, rustling silver light washed everywhere. Her wet cheeks tingled in the wind that whipped her hair and flapped her robe. She walked slowly through the grass, from the house to the garage. The moon's reflection in the windowpane. Back around to the garden again. She stands enveloped by the light.

Garden Primitives

A moon-lit tomato lies at her feet, the smooth skin of the fruit under her arch. Firm. Slow pressure. Giving way. Juice on her ankle. Wet flesh between her toes. She bends her head back and her face meets the sky, meets the silver leaves jostling in the trees. The leaves like the sails of a thousand tiny boats that could, at any time, pull free and set sail into the night.

✦ Garden Primitives

THE GLASS HOUSE STANDS, a refuge in a park on the outskirts of a zoo. The grounds are covered in thigh-deep snow. The sheet-white surface lies unbroken, except for the furrowed tracks of rabbits and the forked imprints left by small birds. People come in frozen cars smudged gray and white with street salt. Their breath catches in the subzero cold like an aerosol shot of dry ice to the lungs. Their bodies constrict inside coats and boots. From the parking lot, they can see the growing green, the seven-foot leaves of tropical trees that press against the glass roof like caged animals. Their footsteps crunch loudly through the thin air. Cold pulls all elements inward, except sound.

Inside the glass house the sounds are of water and the slow murmur of photosynthesis. The warmed air smells of dirt and wet orchids. Sun radiates gold through the canopy of leaves that hang like the lolling heads of dinosaurs. It casts shadows that weave transparently around branches, that squat in the soil beneath low fronds. There are yellow blotches of sun on tree trunks. A pink petal flares. Thin stamens vibrate. A reflecting pool opens around a fountain where water surges from a ring of spouts. The streams both rise and fall at once, tossing clear marbles that drop back to the pond. The sound is continuous. It comes from everywhere.

The woman on the bench is listening. A patch of warm light rests on her lapel. A coin warms in her closed fist. The sound of the fountain keeps changing in her ear. It is static. It is joyous. It is monotony. At her feet, her briefcase is full of demands. She is watching the goldfish at the surface of the pond. Their shocking orange heads break the brown water. They do not move. They float like deadwood. She catches a glimpse of the giant fish. Its back is mottled black, white, and red. It swims with stealth. It disappears like dreaming.

The gray-haired man has a video camera. His eye stays nestled in its black rubber eyepiece. He bends near a spiked-leafed plant and points the lens up the stalk, then pauses at a yellow flounce of blossom. The tape reels inside the machine. Standing, he sees a lavender flower on a tree with leaves that are paper-thin hearts. He shoots the flat leaves, the delicate flower, and inadvertently the pane of glass that divides the warm air from the cold, the green shapes from the plane of white,

Garden Primitives

and the bare oak that stands in the distance. "Vanilla Tree," he whispers its name. Shooting as he walks, he scans the pond and the fountain. He lingers at the statue of St. Francis of Assisi, to whom all creatures were mirrors of God. He frames the stone feet surrounded by moss, the cool folds of the robe, and the thumbless hands. The palms offer a silent welcome. The old man continues around the pond. "Camel Thorn," he whispers, "Common Fig."

In the evening, he will eat a potpie on his sofa and watch his footage on television—St. Francis's smooth cheek and a spray of dark leaves where a porous-skinned orange hangs from a thin stem—while the yellow cat sits on what had been his wife's chair. The old man has a library of video cartridges, every spine labeled in his wobbly hand.

A water drop is falling from a high pane of glass, clear, catching light with gravity's speed. It ticks onto a waxy leaf, then rolls along a green canyon of vein to the leaf's sharp edge, where it hangs and elongates. Falling, a golden thread in the jungle. Clear. Pink. It hits the ground.

The fisted woman on the bench now has light across her sleeve. Her eyes have not strayed from the fountain. She has noticed how the goldfish cluster around it, how their red heads jostle in the divots of water. She looks at her fist, her lacquered nails. Her eyes are staring at her hand, but she is seeing the primate house. She had stood in the darkness of the subterranean hallway facing floor-to-ceiling plexiglass. It was all that divided her from the orangutan that paced its habitat of fake rock and wood. Her eyes see her hand. Her mind sees the ape, its long torso, short legs, its nipples and elbows. It seemed capable of compassion and desire. It had passed so close that she'd seen its fingernails, and its palms that were mapped with lines like her own. She wondered if its captivity could be read there. She wanted to communicate that she was sorry, but the creature took no notice of her. Rubbing her fist against her leg, she now sees fish bobbing in the water. The fountain sounds neither joyous nor monotonous, but quite distinctly inevitable. She checks her watch and reaches for her briefcase. She stands, opening her hand to the nickel, warmed and weighted beyond its five cents. The woman tosses it into the pond and wishes for the strength to be without answers.

The large mottled fish sees a glint of light as the coin tumbles to the bottom of the pool.

The couple walks along the stone path. They step in unison, arms holding each other. The smell of dirt confirms their bodies. Everything conspires to reflect their love. At their feet, a shadow curves like a hip. They gaze at the frilled mouths of orchids, at stems and tufted bark, and subtle greens that are striped with slats of lemon

Garden Primitives

light. At the pond's railing they stop to lean. The warm air is like breath on an ear. They are learning how a pupil eclipses an iris, how hair frames a face that hangs over water. Their coins fall carrying magnanimous wishes, the kind meant for a world or a perfect stranger.

The boy skips past. He doesn't notice the couple. His mother lags behind with a small child on her hip. The boy has seven coins in his pocket. He throws them in the water one after another. He does not wish, he just likes to throw them. The mother is pointing things out to the young one—the colorful flowers, the great big leaves. The boy is a bee going from plaque to plaque. He has learned to read the names of things. "String of Hearts," he calls back to her. "Travelers Tree," his voice is humming. Soon she is struggling her littlest into a snowsuit and digging through a bag for hats and mittens. She tells him they must go home to dinner. The boy protests. The boy waits on a bench. He swings his booted feet in circles. Looking up at a banana tree, he sees helicopter blades in the long thick leaves.

Each day the glass house opens its doors to anyone who wishes to come. They pay fifty cents to the woman at the desk who smiles up at them from her novel. They carry sketch pads, cameras, and books. They leave their coats hanging on hooks in the entry.

The sun is low; it has slipped behind rooftops. The shadows of leaves on the water have vanished. There's a

Garden Primitives

gray cast to the air. A hollowness between tree trunks. A guard checks the premises; keys jangle from his belt. The wind blows snow against the glass. Inside, the plants do not stir.

Some nights the glass house is lit like a prism as wedding vows are spoken or musicians perform. This night the glass house will stand empty, lit only by a three-quarter moon. The moon will trace silver pencil lines over bark and shift slowly across the face of St. Francis. It will shine white on the glossy dracaena, edge its pale flowers that bloom in the night. The sound of the fountain will fill the empty space, pearls of water spilling from infinity's necklace, while the fish sleep and traverse the darkness.

At 7 A.M. the gardening crew will arrive to pull the coiled hoses from the walls. They will set their coffee cups on the stone benches while they talk and pull weeds from the soil. With pole-pruners, they will snip at high branches, or perhaps roll out the hydraulic lift. They will pluck spent flowers that come soft between their fingers and dust the name plaques while a zoo-keeper feeds the fish. And as he does every third morning, the whistling gardener will pull on his waders. With a broom and a dustpan he'll step into the pool. The fish will flee the churning of his broom as he sweeps coins into his pan, a happy song with no name blowing through his teeth.

Garden Primitives

✦ AUTHOR'S ACKNOWLEDGMENTS

support: uphold, sustain, maintain, advocate, champion
inspire: encourage, hearten, induce, motivate, prompt, breathe

I am grateful to the members of the Saturday group: Jeanne Farrar, Jenny Hill, Duke Klassen, Kathy Lewis, Jane Lund, and Pat Rhoades, who have given their thoughtful attention to the evolution of every story in this book. To the steady support of my family, Henry and Georgette Sosin, Michelle, Madeleine, and Phillip. To Patsy Foster-Bolton, the Hunters, Leslie Johnson, Catherine Irmiter, Lucien Orsoni, Sarah Stonich, Alice Templeton, Mike Tillotson, and Suzanne Wolff—all of whom played a role in the creation of this book. And to those of you who are not listed here, but who are in other ways the bread of my life. To the Minnesota State Arts Board for its generous grant. To Norcroft, The Oberholtzer Foundation, Ragdale, The Virginia Center for the Creative Arts for all that residency queen treatment. To the staff at Coffee House Press, especially Chris Fischbach, whose keen editing ear and whose general countenance made working together such a pleasure. To Sarah Fox, who generously introduced my manuscript to Chris. And to Patricia Weaver Francisco, to whom I am the most indebted, who has guided my hand from the very start, giving freely of her love of words, her talent, and her immense heart. Cheers.